Diary of a Teenage Superhero (The Teen
Superheroes Series)

Find out more about Darrell at his website:

http://www.darrellpitt.com

Email: darrellpitt@gmail.com

Dedicated

To Aimee

Teen Superheroes

Book One

Diary Of A Teenage Superhero

Chapter One

My name is—

Wait.

Scrub that thought. I don't know my name. I don't know where I am. I don't know how I came to be here.

I don't know anything.

I'm lying flat on my back looking up at a ceiling coated in peeling mustard yellow paint. Light is streaming in through a window, casting long rectangles across the floor and the bed. A white curtain, fading to brown, covers the window. To its left hangs a small white hand basin. It's leaning badly, clinging grimly to the wall by only one bracket. A single square mirror sits directly above it. A plain round clock to its left counts the minutes.

3.07pm

This place has all the trappings of a seedy motel room. It even smells like it. Stale. Unkempt. Even the mattress smells bad, covered by a grimy gray sheet.

I stagger to the hand basin. My head feels heavy. Everything seems to be vibrating from side to side. I feel like I've been drugged. I look into the mirror.

The face staring back is completely unfamiliar.

But this is me. Male. Seventeen. Maybe eighteen. Short cropped brown hair. Brown eyes. A small scar on the left side of my chin. I'm wearing a blue and white striped t-shirt. Gray jacket. Faded blue jeans. My shoes are clean, though worn.

Then I examine my hands. Not working hands. Not someone who's used to outdoor labor. I'm probably still at school.

Wherever that is.

But I still have one overriding question.

Who am I?

I turn around to survey the room and discover something so unexpected I fall back in surprise and almost dislodge the hand basin completely from the wall.

A man is lying on the floor.

As I was a few minutes earlier, he is face up and staring at the ceiling. Unlike me, he has a wound in his side, possibly a bullet wound. Blood seeps from it. His eyes are open and staring. More blood stains his mouth.

He is lying so close to the bed, I can see why I didn't notice him earlier. Did I do this? Did I harm this man? I don't see a weapon. Regardless, I have to help him in whatever way I can. Kneeling beside him, I gently pull his shirt apart to examine the wound. I don't know wounds—no medical training springs to mind—but it looks bad. I reach into my pocket and find a handkerchief. Pushing it hard against the injury, the man's eyes shift to me.

'It's okay,' I tell him. 'I'm going to get help.'

He shakes his head. Tries to speak. Fails.

'I'll get an ambulance,' I say.

'No,' he responds. 'My…'

His eyes search the ceiling hopelessly. He wants to speak, but the pain is so bad the words will not come. I take his hand.

'I'll get help,' I offer.

The stranger squeezes my hand and before I know it he is dragging it towards his coat pocket. He forces my hand around something hard and rectangular. A book. As I draw it from his pocket he points to me. I know what he's saying.

He wants me to take the book.

I don't care about the book. It can wait. 'I'll get help.'

He shakes his head. With an enormous effort, he takes a deep breath and looks into my eyes.

'Your name is Axel,' he says. 'You have to find the Swan. You can't trust…'

A spasm of pain seizes him and he shudders. For a long moment I think he's going to die. Then the pain seems to subside as his breathing becomes more rapid.

'Trust no-one,' he says. 'Some…at The Agency…will help you. The answer…is in the book.'

'The book?' My mind whirls in confusion.

His hand traces a path across his body and finds its way up my arm. He points with a single finger. There are a series of tiny pinpricks running all the way up my arm. I touch the injuries.

Either someone has injected me…

Or I'm a drug addict.

'The Agency…' He tries to speak again, but the pain must be terrible. A pattern of sweat breaks out across his forehead. I should be finding a doctor for him, but now he grabs my hand again and holds it tight.

'Make…' he begins again.

'Yes,' I say.

'…a difference,' he says. 'Make…'

How I'm supposed to make a difference is a subject that becomes a mute issue. The stranger's head falls back as his hand goes limp and his eyes go unfocused.

He's dead.

I slowly release his hand. The whole incident has been so shocking, so unexpected, so all completely mind numbing that I feel like I've been hit with an electric shock. The man is dead. I've got to find—Who? *The Swan?*

Apart from a type of bird, I have no idea what

or who the Swan could be. And then there's The Agency.

Oh great, I think. *Trust no-one, but at least some people at The Agency* are *on my side. Whatever agency he was referring to.*

I slump next to the dead body and stare blankly at the walls. All my strength is gone. Then slowly I realize there was one other piece of information the stranger imparted to me that was important.

Vitally important, actually.

My name is Axel.

I'm Axel—someone. No last name. No address. I rack my brain. There is a curious blank void that seems to lie outside of my thoughts. Even my own name means nothing to me. It's as foreign as everything else.

I don't remember friends or family. I can remember places. Television programs. Types of food. Lyrics of songs. But as soon as I try to extract personal information about myself—nothing.

The sounds outside the window slowly

intrude. The din of traffic. The faraway whistle of a train. The overhead drone of a passenger jet. Slowly the sounds bring me back to the present. Slowly I realize that I'm now sitting on the floor with the body of a deceased individual. The man's body is cooling. He will never move again under his own volition. At some point in the future he will be laid to rest.

Under normal circumstances I would go to the police, but these are not normal circumstances.

Trust no-one.

That's what he told me. Trust no-one. The book he handed me is sitting on the floor. I tuck it into my back pocket. Then I start a search through the pockets of the dead man. I'm squeamish, but not so squeamish I don't make a thorough job of it.

The only thing I find is a business card. It reads:

Cygnus Industries

Below it is an address on West Forty-Ninth Street in New York City.

A sound comes distantly from within the building; a jarring, clanking din. It can only be an elevator. As I hear it wheeze to a halt, I slowly rise and stare at the door. I have to get out of here. The best course of action is to make some distance between myself and this crime scene. I don't think I'm responsible for this man's death—I don't see a murder weapon—but staying here can only be asking for trouble.

I cross to the door, but at the same time I hear footsteps in the hall outside. They are the tread of more than one individual. Maybe two or three people. Purposeful. Determined. I hear them draw frighteningly close just as I reach for the door handle.

Holding my breath, I don't make a sound.

Someone starts to turn the door handle from the other side.

Chapter Two

The door is locked.

My heart is beating so hard I actually feel slightly faint. The handle turns once. Twice. Jiggles vigorously. I stare at it in horror. Then someone slams into it with their shoulder. The sound of muffled voices emanates from the other side.

Spinning about, my eyes helplessly search the room. There is only a single window and I'm several floors above the street.

Except…

I race to the window and unlock it. There is a fire escape on the other side. I try pushing the window up, but the owner of the building has very intelligently decided to *paint it shut*.

I push up on the sash with all my might. It moves. Slightly. Glancing back to the door, I see it shudder as the strangers on the other side slam against it.

It won't hold.

So I draw back from the window, raise my leg and kick hard at the glass. It shatters and I immediately punch out the remaining jagged shards with my hand. I climb headfirst out onto a fire escape and race to the stairs to my left. Within seconds I'm charging down them as I hear the crash of the opening door from the room above.

There's no time to think. There's only time to act. I don't run as much as fling, scramble and tumble down from one level to the next. I hear something thud onto the escape above me. More footsteps. They're giving chase.

The terror of being caught drives me on faster. I slip on the stairs and bang my knee. The pain is instantaneous; a shooting explosion of agony that dances up and down my leg. I ignore it as a new thought in the back of my mind drives me forward.

If it was the cops at the door, they would have identified themselves as such. So these aren't the cops. Not anyone legal.

So who are they?

There's no time to ponder the question. I take

another turn in the fire escape and find it ends.

My heart nearly stops with panic until I look to my left and see a ladder. Of course. A sliding ladder is attached to the escape to allow residents to evacuate the building, but not to allow thief's access to the apartments at other times. I push the ladder down as hard as I can and it slides easily to the ground.

Seconds later I'm on the street. Once again, there's no time to think. I'm in a wide back alley behind a row of buildings. Large square trash cans line the laneway. I sprint up the length of it as the sound of feet bang loudly on the escape behind me.

I'm halfway down the block when I hear the gunshot. It slams into a wall to my right and I immediately veer away, forcing myself to weave slightly to become a more difficult target. The gun fires again. And again. This time I feel something whiz past my ear. I put on a burst of speed, reach the end and round the corner.

A man and woman holding hands walk past me. They cast a curious glance in my direction.

Probably I'm wild eyed and looking like a crazy person. So be it. *I am a crazy person. Someone is trying to kill me.* I charge across the street. A car screeches. I veer away from it. Another one stops in front of me. I roll across the bonnet.

Gotta keep moving, I tell myself. *Gotta keep—*

Bang!

Bang! Bang!

People start to scream. A shop window explodes. I see a man bend sideways onto the sidewalk.

No!

But I can't stop. If they're prepared to shoot a complete stranger then there's no limit to what they'll do to me. I sprint up the sidewalk and find a thin alley between the buildings. I tear down it, reach the other end and dance about undecided. Left or right? It makes no difference at all because I have no idea where I am. I just need to put distance between myself and my pursuers.

The street is congested with traffic, so I start to cross between the vehicles. There are a couple of trucks idling in the midst of the chaos.

This is part of the afternoon rush hour. Wherever I am. I think it's Manhattan. So many engines are churning at the same time that it takes me a moment to realize I can hear a higher pitched whine above the chaos.

I turn around to see a girl roaring up behind me on a motorcycle. She is slim and dressed in black jeans and a leather jacket. The helmet obscures her face. No sooner do I acknowledge her appearance than I realize her eyes are focused directly on me.

'Get on!' she snaps.

'What?'

'Get on! I'll get you out of here.'

I'm standing undecided in the middle of the traffic. Out of the corner of my eye I see three men round a corner. They are all muscle bound, dressed in identical tank tops and jeans. One of them is holding a gun.

The words go through my mind again as I look at the girl.

Trust no-one.

Turning my back on her, I weave through the cars until I reach the sidewalk. A moment later I'm racing down another narrow side alley. It suddenly occurs to me that the book is still in my back pocket. The stranger in the room died to entrust it to me. Slowing, I spot a gap in the brickwork near the bottom of a wall. I bend over and slide the book in. It fits. In fact, the spine blends so well it could have been made to match.

At the end of the alley I find an empty patch of road and a wide river. I'm on the island of Manhattan. I'm sure of it. I have all of five seconds to process this information before I hear the squeal of brakes.

I race up the road, but within seconds a truck has pulled up beside me. Half a dozen thugs leap out. One of them tackles me to the ground. I try screaming for help, but no-one's around.

They drag me into the van. Something hits me hard just above my right ear. The world goes black.

Chapter Three

The sounds come to me first. A confusing mishmash of words and phrases that make no sense. Opening my eyes I can see only black. Slowly I realize that something is covering my face.

A hood.

I'd like to say the memories come pouring back, but mostly they do not. My name is Axel. That much I know. I remember the dead man in the room and my desperate escape through the streets of Manhattan. I remember the men in the truck.

A shred of knowledge burns the pit of my stomach.

I'm in trouble. Big trouble.

It's the kind that people don't usually survive.

I could die in this place.

At that instant the hood is dragged off my head and I find myself half blinded by the light. My hands are handcuffed to the arm rests of a wooden chair. My ankles are attached to the legs of the chair via more metal restraints.

Disconcertingly, the chair is bolted to the floor.

Blinking into the glare, I find myself in a timber room with bare walls and ripped carpet. It's some kind of derelict building. Angling my eyes upwards I spy a single light set into the ceiling. It is intensely bright. And hot. Must be halogen. It cleanly separates light from dark. A clock hangs on the wall. Ten minutes past six.

I am afraid.

But it is not the room that makes me afraid.

It is the man sitting before me.

He looks emaciated; his suit almost looks like it is ready to fall off. He is narrow faced, bald except for tufts of graying hair above his ears. He has a tiny chin that recedes straight into his neck. His lips are slender and tight. His glasses have round lenses; they are the type that John Lennon made so famous.

He smiles.

I wish he hadn't done that. It is almost reptilian.

'Ah.' His voice is soft and calm. 'You're

awake. I'm so pleased. I was afraid Terrance had struck you so hard you would never speak again.'

I say nothing.

'Speak to me, boy.' The smile has not left his lips. 'What is that old expression? Has the cat got your tongue?'

I slowly shake my head.

'How are you feeling?' He leans forward. 'Is your head sore?'

I nod. When I speak, my voice is a croak. 'Whatever it is you're after, I can't help you.'

He cuts me off with a wave of his hand. 'Save your breath. We are still in the introductory phase. We will become friends. You believe that, don't you? We will be friends?'

Out of all the things I believe at that moment, becoming friends with this man ranks last on the list. Regardless, it is pointless to antagonize him. I nod.

'Good,' he says. 'Now, would you like a drink of water?'

'Yes.'

He rises from the chair, goes to the door and

departs. My first action is to try my restraints. There is a tiny amount of give, but only keys will open the locks. The chair is timber and, given time, I could possibly rock back and forth on the chair and try to collapse the furniture into pieces, but time is a luxury I don't have. The man reappears with a glass of water in his hand. He holds it to my mouth and I drink. After the third swallow I wonder if the liquid could be poisoned, but that could be a blessing depending on what this man has in store for me.

He draws back the empty glass, sits back in the seat and places the glass next to the chair.

'How easily most problems are answered,' he says. 'A man is thirsty. He drinks water and his thirst is quenched. Simple.' He nods. 'My name is Doctor Ravana. As they say on television shows, 'I will be your host for the evening'.'

I nod.

'Questions and answers are similarly simple.' He bites thoughtfully on his bottom lip with his thin, even teeth. 'As long as the questions are answered correctly, honestly, with humility and verisimilitude there are no problems.'

He speaks as if delivering a lecture.

'I will not lie,' I say. 'I have nothing to lie about. I don't know anything.'

'Everyone says that.' He nods, smiling again, but there is no humor in the smile. 'In the beginning.'

'But I really don't know anything,' I say. 'I woke up in a room. I couldn't remember my name.'

'But you remember now,' he interrupts.

'My name is Axel.'

'Good,' he says. 'We have a beginning.'

'But I don't remember how I got there. There was a man in the room. A dead man.'

'His name?' the doctor inquires.

'I don't know,' I say. 'I don't know his name.'

'You see,' he says. 'This is where we have a problem. How does one separate the lies from the truth?' He makes a motion with his hands as if panning for gold. 'It would seem that a person must be not only willing to tell the truth—'

'I am willing,' I say. 'I am telling you the truth!'

'—but desperate to tell me the truth,' he finishes.

For the first time I realize the man has a slight accent. German, I think. He is reminiscent of one of those death camp doctors during the war. The comparison does nothing to ease my mind.

'Desperate,' he repeats.

I say nothing. The silence in the room yawns between us like the sky at night. Open and endless.

'Desperation is a powerful emotion,' he says again. 'It brings things to the surface. It separates the chaff from the grain. You see, it is not enough that you are telling me the truth.'

He leaves the chair, kneels in front of me and places a bony hand on my knee.

'I must *believe* you are telling me the truth.' He nods, looking down as if confirming the thought in his own mind. 'I must believe it.'

'I will tell you the truth,' I start, but already Ravana has risen to his feet and crossed to the door. He leaves the room and a moment later I hear the rumble of a trolley. He reappears with a medical trolley and wheels it into the room. An electrical device sits on the upper level. It is a plain, silver box with two lights. One is green. The other is red.

'Do not be fooled by appearances,' he says. 'This is a highly sophisticated device. And equally effective.'

The device has a hand held wand made from metal. A lead runs from it to the silver box on the trolley.

'I will ask you questions,' he says. 'You will give me answers. The pain from the probe is all consuming. One second of it will seem to last an hour, but fortunately the agony will disappear completely when the probe is removed. In fact, you will feel a strange euphoria. As if you are sitting by the beach on a summer's day.'

'You don't have to do this,' I say desperately. 'I will tell you the truth.'

'I know you will tell me the truth.' He turns the device on and a low hum fills the room. 'They always do.'

Chapter Four

When I awake I find every inch of my body is covered in a lather of sweat. My clothes are drenched. Blood seeps from my bottom lip; I remember biting down on it during the interrogation.

I lift my head slowly. The doctor has left the room.

I want to vomit.

Ravana was right in what he said. When the probe was taken away from my bare skin, the pain instantaneously disappeared, instantly replaced by a sense of relief. Pleasure, even, like being bathed in a tub of warm water.

But when the probe was applied it was like being on fire.

During those minutes the outer world ceased to exist. There was no city. No room. No chair. There was only Ravana and the probe.

And his questions. His voice calmly asking me again, and again.

'Where is the headquarters of The Agency?'

'I don't know.'

'Where is The Swan?'

'Please, I don't know where he is. I don't even know who he is.'

'What was the name of the dead man in the room?'

'I don't know.'

'His name? You must know his name?'

'Please, I don't know.'

Ravana is gone. It is only now I look up at the clock. It is almost seven o'clock. I have been in the room for less than an hour, but he has broken me. I would have condemned my own grandmother to death if he had asked me. Anything to avoid the all consuming pain of the probe. But I could not tell him anything.

I don't *know* anything.

Then I remember the book. In the midst of the interrogation there was no mention of the book or any questions about the man giving me anything. I know I will tell Ravana about the book. It is still hidden in the wall in the alley. I will take him to the book, if necessary. Anything to avoid the pain.

A bottomless void fills my stomach. Deep down inside I know that even if I comply with every direction given to me I will probably not survive this experience. Ravana is no amateur. His calm demeanor has convinced me he has tortured many other people and he always gets his way. He did not lose his temper once during the interrogation. Didn't even raise his voice. He was the picture of calm.

I will tell him about the book.

Footsteps rebound in the hallway outside. He enters with a spring in his step as if he has just returned from taking a stroll outside. His face brightens into a smile.

'Ah, you've awoken,' he says. 'Wonderful. I was concerned you would sleep for hours.'

'Please,' I say. 'I will speak. I don't know anything, but I've just remembered something.'

At that moment I hear a rapid *pop, pop, pop*.

The smile fades from Ravana's face. 'What is happening?'

He turns back to the door and the sound of a

man screaming reverberates along the corridor. Ravana grabs the door and pushes it shut. I derive more than a little pleasure in seeing him stand nervously behind the door, staring at it defensively. He reminds me of a naughty child waiting nervously for punishment from an angry parent.

More screaming comes from beyond the door. More firing of guns. I hear a sound like punches being thrown and then a final crash as a body hits the ground. A full minute passes. Ravana stands fearfully behind the door, clenching his fist.

'This is not possible,' he says. 'They cannot find us!'

The door is smashed open. Ravana staggers backwards as he defensively raises his fists. A person enters the room. It is a girl. Slowly I recognize her. It is *the* girl I saw on the motorcycle earlier. The one who ordered me to go with her.

She glances at me. 'Bet you wish you'd accepted the ride.'

I nod dumbly.

The girl turns back to Ravana. The torturer

suddenly looks like a cornered rat. His eyes dart around the room as if willing the walls to grow another door. Finally his gaze settles on the girl.

'Hurting me would be an enormous mistake,' he says.

'Not hurting you would be a bigger one,' she replies.

Faster than the eye could see, her fist snakes out and hits Ravana across the chin. He hits the ground like a sack of potatoes. My mouth falls open. I've never seen anyone move so fast.

The girl examines the chair. An instant later she has broken the arm rest on one side and my hand is free. I am wearing the handcuff like a bracelet, but my arm is free. She repeats the action on the other arm rest and for a finale breaks the legs with a couple of kicks. Producing a small piece of metal she quickly and efficiently picks the locks of the cuffs. They fall free.

'Let's get out of here,' she says.

'You'll get no arguments from me.' I follow her. 'Can you at least tell me your name?'

'It's Brodie,' she says.

I notice something about the way she says it. I realize she has an accent. I decide to ask about her country of origin later.

In the hallway there are groaning and bleeding men all over the floor. I vaguely recognize some of them from when I was grabbed. To my surprise, we start to head upstairs. I don't argue. It's when we reach the roof of the building that I look around in confusion.

'What're we doing up here?'

'I'm pretty sure more reinforcements are arriving,' Brodie says. 'I can handle a lot of them by myself, but I can't protect you at the same time.'

'So how do we get off here?'

'We jump.'

'Jump?'

'Sure. It's only to the next roof.' She starts across the roof. 'It's not too far.'

Okay, time for a reality check. Jumping from building to building might be something Mrs Bruce Lee does on a daily basis, but it's a little out of my league. We reach the edge of the roof. With every step my legs shake a little more. By the time we can see the streets below they're quivering like jelly. There *is* a building next to us, but it's not simply a small step. It must be at least eight feet away.

I can't do it. I still can't remember my past, but I do realize something about myself that I didn't know before now.

I'm terrified of heights.

'You'll have to trust me,' she says. 'We're going to take a long run up and then jump across.'

'There's part of that I don't understand.'

'Which part?'

'Everything after, 'you'll have to trust me'.' I look down at the alley below. *'Have you lost your mind?* Jumping? Are we talking the same language? I'm going down via the stairs. I'm not jumping anywhere.'

She starts to argue with me, but I'm already making my way back to the stairwell. I'm about to enter when I hear the hammering of steps on the stairs below. Someone—correction—a lot of someones are racing up the stairs.

Hell.

I turn around just in time to see Brodie in mid flight. Obviously she has decided to shame me into jumping from one building to the next, but she has failed to inspire me with her bravado. I see her land and roll. A second later she's back on her feet, waving to me.

Come on!

I glance down the stairwell. The cacophony of feet is drawing closer. I can try to jump or I can remain here to be interrogated again by Ravana.

I run towards the edge of the roof on shaking legs. I pick up speed quickly, though and accelerate. It's not such a big distance and I will be across before I know it. The one thing I don't notice is the small lip on the edge of the roof. It's only a few inches high. I only see it out of the corner of my eye it at the last second. By then it's too late.

My foot catches on it and instead of a graceful leap, I trip and sprawl out into space. Brodie's mouth opens in horror. My arms stretch out. Brodie screams.

The roof of the building opposite disappears from view.

I fall between the buildings.

Chapter Five

My forward momentum takes me as far as the opposite wall. I hit it with both hands. My nails rake the brick work, but don't find purchase. My lower body collides a moment later.

Then gravity takes hold.

To make matters worse, for every action there's an equal and opposite reaction, so my impact against the wall results in a slight rebound. As I fall I see something a few feet below my hands.

I reach out with everything I've got and one hand grabs the top of a window frame. My body swings towards the building.

Crash!

I hurtle through a window and into someone's living room. It isn't a graceful landing. Far from it. But it's a landing. And I've only fallen a few feet as opposed to a hundred feet, so it's a win as far as I'm concerned.

I'm covered in glass, timber and shredded curtain. Picking myself up, I find I've destroyed someone's flower pot and knocked over their television set. An elderly black woman is sitting on her lounge looking at me with open mouthed astonishment. I can't blame her. It's not every day a teenage boy comes smashing through her window.

Bang!

A bullet thuds into the carpet next to my face.

Someone's shooting at me!

'Sorry about this,' I climb to my feet.

She stands up, waving a finger at me and yelling something unintelligible.

I charge through her apartment and, more by chance than design, find the front door. Just as I struggle to open the lock something hits me from behind. Hard. I turn around and a broom smacks me in the face. Grabbing hold of the old lady's weapon, I get the door open and stumble into the hallway.

'And don't come back!' she yells.

Those words I understand.

I'm in the middle of a long hallway in a rundown apartment building. A door has opened down the passage and a young mother and her son peer out in astonishment. I realize part of the curtain is still hanging off my shoulder. Knocking it to the ground I try to wave reassuringly.

'It's okay,' I tell them. 'Knocked over a vase.'

I hurry in the opposite direction to a set of elevators. I'm about to hit the down button when I notice they're already ascending. But is this good news? This could be Ravana's men. Could they be that fast?

I spot a set of fire stairs to my left. Dragging open the door, I start down them. There is a gap I can look down and see all the way to the bottom. It looks to be about ten stories. I hurry down one set of winding stairs and pass the door leading from that level. That's one floor gone. Only about nine to go. Racing down another two floors I suddenly notice a sound and stop.

Footsteps.

Or am I just imagining it?

Is it just the reverberation of my own feet? Silence fills the stairwell. Regardless, I have to keep going. I continue down another floor, slow down and listen. Sounds okay. I rush down another floor and hurry past the entry door from that level.

The door flies open.

The guy catches me from the side, throwing me towards the railing and knocks the air out of me. He is tall and thin with a cruel face. He gets an arm around my throat and drags me backwards.

'We're not finished with you, kid,' he says. 'The doctor's got a long night of fun planned for you.'

It's the reminder of Doctor Ravana that does it. I see the doctor's face in my mind and his patient expression as he applies the probe to my hand. If there's one thing I know for sure, it's that I never want to return to that room again.

Bringing my elbow up into his stomach I hear a satisfying *oomph* and his grip loosens. Slightly. But not enough to escape. So I repeat the action three or four times more just to get the point across. All the while we're sliding and stumbling down the steps. I swing around and brace him against the railing while I slam my elbow into his diaphragm.

I turn around and blindly swing a fist into his jaw.

It happens suddenly. The railing is not that high. Probably some building inspector looked at it thirty years ago and gave it a green light without a second thought. Little did he think this little piece of building design would become the stage of a *life and death battle*.

Because at that instant the thin man falls backwards. If it weren't so horrifying it would be funny because he actually flips back like some sort of character in a comedy show. I make a grab for him, but the angle is bad and all I grab is a part of his jacket. It tears out of my grasp and he disappears from sight.

I watch him fall down the gap between the stairs. It seems to take forever. He gives an inarticulate cry. Makes a sound that has no meaning. At some stage his eyes meet mine during that endless fall. It's almost an expression of disbelief.

How can you be responsible for my death?

Then he hits the ground floor with a terrible

splat. Open mouthed, I stare down at his motionless form. Maybe he's not dead.

Please God, let him not be dead.

I stumble down the remaining flights of stairs in a daze. I slip over twice, but barely notice. All I can think of are the man's eyes. Such sheer disbelief. He must be alive. He can't be dead. People survive falls worse than that and survive.

Finally I reach the final turn in the stairs. The thin man lies in a growing pool of blood. The shape of his body is like some sort of crooked swastika. His disbelieving eyes are dull with death.

I have killed him.

I have just killed a man.

Chapter Six

It is evening. The air grows cooler by the minute. Shops and apartment buildings slide past my gaze. Cars beep at each other. Someone practices opera from an open window. A man sweeps his front step with a straw broom.

I see and hear it all, but it is as if I am deaf and blind.

I have killed a man.

I am a murderer.

It was self defense. That goes without saying. There is no doubt in my mind the man would have dragged me back to the room with Doctor Ravana and I would have been tortured and eventually killed. My body would have probably been buried in an unmarked grave or disposed of in a river. My parents, whoever they are, would never know what had happened to me. My own death would have been a foregone conclusion if I had been recaptured.

Still, I have killed a man and I will carry that knowledge with me for as long as I live. This is what soldiers must go through. They must experience similar feelings of guilt and horror. Once a person passes through that door they can never return. I have taken a human life and there will never be a time when that can be undone.

Every time I close my eyes I see the event in some sort of stop motion sequence. I try to grab him. He falls. His eyes meet mine. His body lies motionless on the floor. His neck lies at an unnatural angle.

Shivering, I wrap my arms around myself. I realize I am cold. Freezing. I stop at a street corner and the city slowly comes to life around me. A man is walking a dog. A woman is playing with her two small children on the sidewalk. A bus stops and passengers exit. It seems inconceivable that people are still carrying out their everyday lives.

I have to start thinking about where to go from here. My eyes randomly search the street and settle on a dimly lit vertical sign.

LIBRARY

Such places often stay open later than many

retail shops. Crossing the road, I mount the steps and a moment later the warm interior embraces me. It's not a large library. More of a local community center. Still, it is better than nothing. An idea is forming in my mind. The woman at the desk smiles at me pleasantly. She is middle aged with brown hair and eyes. Probably even if you saw her on the street, you would still pick her profession. They must make all librarians from the same cookie mold.

'I'm sorry to bother you,' I say. 'I'm very lost. I was on the tourist bus and I've gotten out at the wrong place.'

She nods.

'Can you tell me where I am?'

'You're on Fort Washington Avenue.'

'Which city?'

She gives me an odd look. 'New York City, of course.'

'Thanks.'

I turn around and meander through the dozen aisles that make up the library. Why am I in New York City? Does my family live here? I find I can remember images of the city, but they could be from television programs. I can't actually remember any street in detail, whether it be from here or anywhere else in the country.

The questions remain: who am I and how did I get here?

I slowly decide on a course of action.

'Can I use your internet?' I ask the woman at the desk.

She looks up. 'Our internet isn't working. I'm sorry.'

She looks a little annoyed. Maybe she's busy playing Minesweeper. I persevere anyway.

'Where are your encyclopedias?' I ask.

She nods towards a nearby shelf. A few minutes later I'm searching the 'S' volume. The man back at the room told me I had to find the Swan. He did not tell me to find *Mr* Swan. I had to find *The* Swan. Possibly the name is some sort of code. Maybe something in the encyclopedia will give me a clue.

Fifteen minutes later I put the book down in frustration. I've found out a lot about swans. They're part of the same family that includes geese and ducks. They are among the largest flying birds in the world. They feature in the mythology of many different cultures.

Unfortunately none of this is going to help. If someone gives me a snap test on swans I should ace it, but as far as finding out what the hell is going on—

I drag open the encyclopedia again. There must be something in here that will help. I'm halfway through studying the section again when something leaps at me from the first line:

Swan (Genus *Cygnus*)

That's the second time today I've seen the word *Cygnus*. The business card I extracted from the dead man's pocket bore the company name *Cygnus Industries*. The address was West Forty-Ninth Street. I sit the book down in triumph. At last I have a lead. The Swan must be located at Cygnus Industries.

'We're closing soon,' the woman calls from her desk.

The woman is becoming icier by the moment. She must have bombed out of Minesweeper. Still, I bravely ask her for directions and within minutes I've found my bearing. Despite everything I've been through, I now have a spring in my step. An hour before I was cold, alone and lost.

Okay, I'm still cold and alone, but at least now I'm not quite so lost. I have a plan. The man in the room said to find the Swan. The Swan can probably tell me all sorts of information, like my last name, my address and how the hell I got into this situation.

I'm feeling brighter by the moment. Maybe I'll even get my memory restored. This time tomorrow I could be with family and friends and looking back on this whole experience as an unpleasant memory.

It only takes me a few minutes to find the right address on West Forty-Ninth Street. It turns out to be an art deco apartment building nestled between taller, more modern structures. Turn of the century apartment blocks huddle together across the road. A motley collection of small businesses seem to operate out of the address. I can see signage in one window for a mortgage broker. Another window advertises shoe repairs.

My eyes slowly shift to the roof of the building. A shape seems to be silhouetted against the night sky. For an instant I think it's a bird, but then I realize it is growing closer with every passing second. Before I can make a move, it becomes terrifyingly close and the object slams into the roof of the car parked behind me. Glass and metal fly in all directions. A passing woman screams and faints. An elderly couple stare in horror at the sight.

I stare in horrified fascination at the dead man. He is covered in blood and more is appearing with every passing second. I can see his face. He looks stunned. Obviously death was the furthest thing from his mind when he reported to work this morning.

Nobody needs to tell me his identity. This is the Swan. As surely as night follows day he is the man who held the answers to all my questions and now those answers have died with him.

One thing I know for certain.

This swan could not fly.

I look back up at the building and get my

second shock for the evening. There is a man leaning out of a window high above. His hands are on the sill. He peers down, not at the dead man on the car, but at me. Our eyes meet.

Doctor Ravana's face twists into an expression of seething hatred.

Chapter Seven

A hand suddenly grabs mine. I'm jolted out of my astonishment by a familiar face, a person who is not looking at me with hate or a maniacal desire to kill me.

'Brodie,' I say.

'I thought I might find you here.'

'How—?'

'Now's not the time,' she interrupts. 'Looks like we're too late to find Mr Swan.'

'You know about him?'

She shakes her head. 'Later.'

We hurry down the street and through a confusion of back alleys and main roads until we've put some distance between us and Ravana. It can't happen soon enough for me. We hurry through a district surrounded by abandoned factories and high fences. It starts to rain and within minutes I'm feeling cold and wet. A distant roll of thunder reverberates around the buildings like the beating of an enormous drum.

'Where are we going?' I ask.

'I've got a place.'

'Where is it? Underwater?'

She gives me an odd look. 'What makes you say that?'

'You're English, aren't you? You know, bad weather and cups of tea?'

'No,' she says. 'I think I'm Australian.'

'You don't remember?'

'Later.'

She flashes me a smile. For the first time I realize she is quite attractive. She has red hair, blue eyes and a neat, heart shaped face. She is still wearing the same clothing—jeans and a jacket.

'Where is this place?' I ask.

'It's close.'

'What happened to your motorcycle?'

'It ran out of fuel.'

'And you didn't get more because…'

'Because I have no money and I didn't feel like robbing a bank to get some.'

Under these crazy circumstances this seems

like a reasonable explanation. She takes a right turn under a gap in a wire fence. I follow her across a vacant lot littered with refuse. We reach a double wooden door secured with a chain. Dragging on the bottom edge, she creates a gap for me to enter.

Whatever the warehouse used to be was a long time ago. There are pieces of machinery all over the place; it's odd looking apparatus not much larger than a person. I suspect that it belonged to the last business run here. Probably this place has held many different commercial enterprises over the years.

'They used to make shoes here,' Brodie says.

'And before that?' I ask. The high ceilings are almost fifty feet above the floor. There's a crane and pulley system that runs the whole length of the structure.

'That's anyone's guess.'

Now the storm has begun in earnest and it's raining hard. Through the glass skylights in the ceiling I can see lightning flash. Its stark light floods the many dark recesses of the warehouse. There are other corners which remain in pitch darkness. Those are the ones that scare me.

'We're safe here,' Brodie says. 'I've been here a while.'

'How long is a while?'

She shrugs. 'About three days.'

'You don't have a home?'

Brodie shakes her head and leads me towards a small office at the rear of the warehouse. She lights a candle and its flickering glow reveals a couple of piles of blankets, a few tins of food, some bottles of water and a few books.

'This is home,' she says. 'Ever since I landed...here.'

'You mean...' I try to understand exactly what she is saying. 'Um, what do you mean?'

'I woke in a building on the other side of town,' Brodie says. 'I had no idea who I was or how I got there or where I came from. I assumed I'd been in an accident and so I started looking for a police officer.'

'Makes sense.'

'I had only walked about a hundred feet down

the street when a van pulled up behind me. These guys jumped out and tried to drag me into the van.'

My blood goes cold. It was bad enough for me, but I can only imagine it would be every woman's worst nightmare. Brodie sees the look on my face and forces a laugh.

'It's okay. They got more than they bargained for.'

'What did you do?'

She throws a few punches into the air. She's fast. Incredibly fast. *Unnaturally* fast. I don't think I realized her speed when she faced Doctor Ravana back in the room. She drops low and kicks into the air. Leaping to her feet, she snatches up a piece of timber from a nearby pile and tosses it up. A second later her hand snakes out and strikes the center of it.

It shatters into matchsticks. I pick up a clutch of the shattered remains and examine it carefully.

'Remind me not to start any arguments,' I say.

'I only use my super powers for good,' she says with a straight face.

'But seriously, that's not normal.'

Fast is fast, but she's so fast I doubt any martial arts expert on Earth could keep up with her. And not only is she quick, but she knows what she's doing too.

'I think I'm about three times as fast as a martial arts expert,' she says. 'Maybe faster.'

'Do you know what style you're fighting in?'

'Style?'

'Kung Fu, jujitsu…'

'Oh, that.' She shakes her head. 'Not a clue.'

'And what about your name?' I ask. 'How did you work out your name?'

'It's on my clothing.'

I suddenly realize my clothing might be similarly marked. I check the inside back of my jeans and—hey presto! The name 'Axel' is stitched onto a small label. I then proceed to tell Brodie about waking up in the room, the guy on the floor and everything that had happened to me since I woke. She listens in dead silence until I finish. Then she just shakes her head in amazement.

'Good thing I've been following those guys

for days. Otherwise…' She lets the word hang in the air. Finally she says, 'That book must be important. It might answer all our questions.'

'We can find it in the morning,' I tell her. 'I know where I left it.'

She nods. 'We'd better get some shut eye. We'll start out early.'

Brodie hands me blankets and a pillow. I don't expect to sleep, but by the time she blows out the candle I find I can barely keep my eyes open. The storm subsides to a steady flow of rain. The wind blows distantly and a piece of metal bangs out a random tune.

The next thing I know is Brodie's shaking me awake. At first I don't know where I am. There is a cramp in my neck and I feel stiff and cold. I look up at her face and don't immediately recognize her. Then it all comes back.

Oh. That's right. Mrs Bruce Lee.

Time to move.

It's early morning. Brodie produces a spare sweater. I'm glad of it because it's a cold morning.

We're out the door in minutes. The rain has stopped, but the streets are still wet. We walk a couple of blocks. Then Brodie spots a nice car. She produces a wire coat hanger from her jacket.

My eyes desperately examine nearby apartments. 'What are you doing?'

'Getting us a ride,' she says. The car door opens and within minutes she has the vehicle hotwired and we're driving through the early morning city streets. I'm shaking my head in amazement. Whatever Brodie was before she arrived here, she was no girl scout. Still, I'm not about to criticize her. Without her we would be walking twenty blocks. Now we cover the same distance in a fraction of the time.

After a while I tell her to pull over. We climb out of the car and make our way down an alley. In the next street I recognize a couple of landmarks. A café. A diner. A used bookshop. This is the place.

Heading down another alley, my eyes search the brickwork. We end up at the other end and slowly work our way back again. I'm beginning to think

Ravana's men have already found the book, but then I notice a shadow near the ground. Easing the book out of the slot, I breathe a sigh of relief. It appears undamaged.

Opening it, I start leafing through the pages. Brodie looks at my face as slowly my expression turns from excitement to disbelief.

'What is it?' she asks finally. 'What's written in it?'

'That's the problem,' I say. 'Nothing's in it. All the pages are blank.'

Chapter Eight

We stare at each other in stunned amazement. Brodie takes the notebook from me and turns over the pages one at a time. She even holds the pages up to the light to see if any words have been etched onto the paper.

'You're sure the book is important?' she asks skeptically.

'Absolutely. The man dragged it out of his pocket with his dying breath and forced it on me.'

Brodie nods. 'Okay, let's head back to the car.'

We return to the vehicle and spend the next half an hour in the front seat examining the book from front to back. At the same time it grows lighter in the street outside. People walk past the vehicle on their way to work. A street cleaning machine zooms down the road. A café owner starts setting out tables and chairs onto the sidewalk. Another day in the Big Apple.

Finally Brodie puts the book down between

the seats. 'The book is a dead end. For now.'

'What do you suggest?'

She thinks for a moment. 'What about Cygnus Industries? We could go back to see what we can find.'

I raise an eyebrow. 'To see what we can find? You mean, like bad guys with guns and psycho doctors? You might have super powers, but—'

'I don't have super powers,' Brodie starts. 'Well, actually I sort of do, but that's beside the point. I still think Cygnus Industries is the safest place for us right now.'

'How do you figure that?'

'They're probably turning this city upside down looking for us,' Brodie explained. 'Cygnus Industries is the last place they'd expect us to return.'

I can't fault her logic. It seems so unlikely we would return there that it's probably the one place we should go. I nod.

'Okay. But you're Batman if the bad guys turn up.'

She smirks. 'Okay, boy wonder.'

We drive across town to Cygnus Industries. Taking care to park some way down the block, we approach the address carefully. The body and the damaged car are long gone, of course. All that remains is a little broken glass on the road. We stroll past it nonchalantly and enter the main lobby. It's an older building, but clean and well maintained. We make straight for the elevators and reach the floor without incident.

The door to Cygnus Industries has been broken open; the lock is hanging on by a single screw. Obviously the men who attacked our contact didn't bother knocking. A zigzag of police tape is strung across the front. No sound comes from within. Silently, we push the door open and ease our way between the police tape. We close the door behind us.

'Wow,' says Brodie.

Wow, indeed. Imagine a fairly typical office with filing cabinets, desks, computers and partitions. Now imagine it has been turned upside down and every file and piece of paper taken. Desks upturned. Computers smashed. Even the water dispenser had been pulled off the wall.

'They obviously don't have a cleaner,' I say.

We start to methodically search every filing cabinet and desk for papers and find—nothing. Not a single page has been left behind. We even start lifting furniture and still find nothing. Not a business card. Zilch. There is a smaller room that leads off the main office of Cygnus Industries. Possibly it was the manager's office as all it contains is a desk and a wardrobe. We search the drawers of the desk and still find nothing.

I try plugging in one of the computers, but it simply gives me a blue screen. It doesn't even start to boot up.

'Holy hell,' I groan. 'This place has been stripped clean.'

'Wait a second,' Brodie holds up a hand. 'Did you hear that?'

We both freeze. I realize Brodie is referring to the elevator. It sounds like the doors are closing. We look at each other. If someone is coming to this office there are frighteningly few places to hide. There is the desk in the manager's office which can fit about half a body under it. Then there's the wardrobe behind it.

We quickly scoot into the office and climb into the wardrobe. Standing there with the door slightly ajar, I peer out to see if anyone enters the main office. At the same time I'm conscious of how close I am to Brodie. She is only a few inches away. My eyes stray to her face. Her lips.

She whispers. 'Keep your mind on the job.'

I avert my eyes. At that same moment I hear the front door to the office creak open. A shuffle of feet. Someone clears their throat. The drawer of a filing cabinet is eased open. More footsteps.

Finally someone steps into view. It's a kid a couple of years younger than me. He is of Asian appearance. Maybe fourteen or fifteen. Black hair. Round face. A bit overweight. He looks completely focused on carrying out the same identical search we have just completed.

I catch Brodie's eye. The whole thing is bizarre. To make matters worse, I know it's only a matter of time before he enters the manager's office and opens the cupboard to find us! A horrible thought goes through my mind. It's terrible, but I can't help it. *No, no, no.* That's too awful. Do not even think about it.

Because all of a sudden I can imagine myself leaping out of the cupboard and scaring the daylights out of the kid. A smile creases my lips.

Brodie looks at me, frowning and I simply shake my head.

Don't worry.

I'm one of the good guys.

At that moment things take a slightly radical turn. The kid suddenly freezes. At first I think he has heard us in the wardrobe. Then I hear a grunt and I see the kid race for the door. Two men crash tackle him to the ground. He hits the ground.

My stomach turns over. One of the men punches the kid hard in the stomach and I see him roll up like an injured bug. The men lift him to his feet, drag him into the office and throw him on the manager's desk. One of them holds him down while the other one navigates around the desk. The man has his back to us; he is so close we could reach out and touch him.

'You're gonna tell us everything you know about The Agency,' the man says.

'Please,' he gasps. 'I don't know anything!'

'You'll speak or—'

That's as far as the man gets. At that moment Brodie pushes open the door of the wardrobe and taps the man on the shoulder. He turns around in astonishment.

'Surprise,' she says.

Chapter Nine

Ten minutes later we're walking down the middle of the sidewalk back towards the car. There is only one word the kid seems capable of saying and now he's saying it a lot.

'Amazing,' he shakes his head. 'Just amazing.'

'You'll get used to it,' I say. 'She's like Bruce Lee. Only better. And faster. And prettier.'

'All in a day's work.' Brodie flashes a smile. 'Now, we'd better start with introductions. What's your name?'

He looks down. 'I wish I could tell you, but I can't.'

'Amnesia?' I ask.

'How'd you know?'

'It's going around,' I say. 'But there's a cure.'

'There is?'

I check the back of his jeans. It turns out his name is Dan.

'I christen you Dan,' I say. 'A last name costs

extra. Now, tell us what you remember.'

He does. It's more similar to Brodie's story than my own. He woke up the previous day in an abandoned shop on the West side of Manhattan with no memory of his previous life. He wandered around aimlessly for a while before realizing he had a piece of paper in his pocket. Nothing was written on the paper, but it had a letterhead.

Cygnus Industries.

He would have gone to the police, but there was something that stopped him. Dan produces a folding knife from his pocket and shows it to us. It has blood on it.

'You don't think—' I begin.

Dan shrugs. 'I didn't know what to think. This isn't my blood so whose is it? Did I stab someone? Did I kill them?' He stops. 'I decided to lay low until I had some answers.'

'I know you don't remember anything much,' Brodie says. 'But you can obviously speak English. Can you speak any other languages?'

He frowns. 'I'm not sure.'

'Say 'my name is Dan' in Japanese,' Brodie instructs.

'I can't.'

'Vietnamese.'

'No.'

'Chinese?'

He lets out a string of words.

'Holy hell,' he says softly. 'I can speak Chinese.'

It's not so much his Chinese that impresses me, but his English. His English is good. Very good. He speaks with a very slight singsong inflection. Otherwise there's no doubt he has spoken the language for a good many years.

'You know,' he muses. 'I can remember streets too. Streets that are not from around here.'

'Are they in China?' I ask.

'I think so,' he says thoughtfully.

Now that he mentions remembering places other than here, my own mind begins to drift. An image comes to me as clear as day. A golden brown field of wheat. Blue sky. A farm house.

The image fades.

It's the first time something has come back to me from my past life, from the time pre-now. I try to recover more of the thoughts—places, names and people—but nothing comes.

Dan continues. 'I might have lived in America for years.'

That's when the shot rings out. It *pings* off a street light next to my head. We swing around. *Damn.* The two guys that Brodie took out of the equation back at Cygnus Industries are charging down the street after us. We run. Another bullet whistles past us. I spy a set of steps leading down into a subway. Pointing towards them, we take the stairs two at a time. There are turnstiles at the bottom. We push through these and hurry down another flight of stairs.

These lead to the station. A train has just pulled in. It lies about fifty feet in front of us. We race down the platform. The doors begin to close. I hold them open as Dan and Brodie squeeze in between them. The train starts to ease out of the station.

Yes!

I punch the air.

'We made it,' Brodie beams. 'Now if—'

The sound of gunfire is explosive and all consuming. I shove Brodie and Dan to the floor as I catch a glimpse of three men on the platform. The two men from the Cygnus office have been joined by a third man. He is holding a machine gun and raking the carriage with fire. Glass explodes everywhere. People dive to the floor. The front cabin where the driver sits implodes inwards with shrapnel. Then the train picks up speed and disappears into the tunnel.

The carriage is relatively empty. The few people inside were scattered around the interior. Now they slowly pick themselves up off the floor. As far as I can see, through some miracle, no-one has been injured. Then I turn my attention to the driver. The door behind the driver contains a small glass panel through which I can see the interior.

The driver is slumped backwards over his seat.

Hell.

'What is it?' Dan asks.

'The driver's dead,' I tell him.

The train continues to pick up speed as one of the passengers appears.

'What's happening, son?'

'It looks like the driver's dead.'

'Holy hell.'

'And we seem to be picking up speed.'

'Surely there's a failsafe switch.'

That would make sense. 'Maybe it was damaged in the gunfire.'

'It's not going to be possible to open that door to get in,' Brodie says. 'We should move everyone towards the back of the train.'

The man nods and starts directing passengers towards the next carriage. It strikes me that people are amazingly supportive of each other in a crisis. The train picks up even more speed. It begins to rock from side to side.

'We'd better get to the back of the train,' Brodie says. 'We can't do anything here.'

We start to move back, but Dan remains at the tiny square of glass, his eyes fixed on the driver. I grab his arm.

'We can't do anything for the driver,' I tell him gently.

'I know.' Dan glances up at me. 'Although I think I might be able to help.'

The train comes out of the tunnel and barrels along an elevated rail line. Apartment buildings fly past on both sides. I feel a real sense of fear. With the speed increasing, even with the people taking refuge in the rear, it's going to be an almighty accident when it happens. A disaster. My heart is beating like a drum. We are not just simply going to slide sedately off the rails. We're going to fly off this elevated line at high speed.

'What do you mean?' Brodie asks.

Dan stands back from the door and holds out his hands. He looks like a magician doing a magic trick. For a moment I wonder if he's completely lost his marbles. Then I notice the door shuddering. It's not just caused by the movement of the train. It's more than that.

It's Dan.

He's doing it with his mind.

Chapter Ten

The hinges start to bend outwards. The door itself even starts to curve towards us as if a giant hand were angling it away from the frame. I glance at Dan. Sweat has broken out on his brow. His hands are shaking. I'm not sure how he's doing this, but somehow he's achieving the impossible. Brodie stares at him wide-eyed. Finally the hinges snap and the door floats free.

That's right.

Floats free.

It lurches to one side and settles against the wall. Dan drops his hands. There are a million things I want to say, but there's no time. I stumble into the driver's cabin. I try to ignore the blood spattered remains of the driver. The scenery outside races past the window.

I find it hard to think. We're hurtling along at a terrific speed. The whole carriage is shuddering violently from one side to the other. I don't know which control to manipulate.

Then I see it. The mechanism is obvious now that I recognize it. It's a dead man's switch, made to only operate when the driver's hand is on it. But a bullet has driven itself into the metal housing, locking it into place. I grab it and pull back. At first nothing happens. Then it suddenly gives, dropping back to the off position. The train begins to slow.

The passenger vehicle is still rocking wildly from side to side, but at least now it doesn't seem to be in danger of flying off the tracks. Just as well, too, because at that moment we're heading for a bend. The train continues to decelerate. Finally as it reaches the bend it gives a final lurching shudder and comes to a halt.

Until then I've been holding my breath. I let it out as Brodie grabs my arm.

'Well done,' she says.

'Well done?' I reply. 'I'm not the one who deserves congratulations.'

We both look back at Dan still standing in the vestibule area. He looks sort of embarrassed. We clap him on the back.

'Do you want to explain all that?' I ask.

'I wish I could,' he says. 'I noticed it not long after I woke up. I was sitting on a park bench watching a coin on the pavement. I thought of how that would be handy to have some money. Suddenly it started sliding towards me. I thought I was possessed.' He gives a nervous laugh. 'After some practice I realized I could move metal objects. I started with small things like coins and later moved onto larger objects.'

'And you didn't mention this to us?' Brodie asks. 'The reason being…'

'I didn't want to seem like a weirdo.' Dan shrugs.

'You're not a weirdo,' I say. 'You're a damn…superhero.'

'You're super…Dan,' Brodie finishes lamely.

'Super Dan,' he says. 'That's great. Real catchy.'

I shake my head. 'Let's worry about names later. I think we should get out of here. I don't want us to try explaining this to the authorities.'

We make our way down the length of the train. It looks like the fire brigade, ambulance and police have turned up. A ladder extends to the elevated line and people are being helped down one at a time. When it comes to our turn we get to street level, but it turns out the police have grouped the passengers together for questioning.

A police officer starts directing people towards a diner. Obviously they intend to personally interview everyone as to the events on the train. I nervously look for an opportunity to escape, but the only way out of here would seem to be breaking free of the group and running at full pelt down the road.

Not a sensible plan.

Everyone is crowded into the diner. We position ourselves into a booth at the end. After a few minutes a man comes over to talk to us. I recognize him as the one we spoke to on the train.

'You three seem a little quiet,' he says.

'Uh, yeah,' Brodie says. Then, 'What do you mean?'

'It was you kids on the train who stopped it,'

he says. 'You saved everyone. Why don't you just tell the cops?'

We look at each other in silence.

Finally I speak. 'We'd rather keep a low profile. We don't want to attract attention to ourselves.'

The man nods, giving it some thought. 'I suppose we owe you all our lives. If that's how you want it to be…'

'It is.'

'Okay.' The man looks over towards the counter. 'There's probably an exit through the kitchen. You'll just have to go round the serving area. If there were a diversion you might be able to leave.'

'What are you suggesting?' Dan asks.

The man glances at the two cops at the door. 'Just be ready for anything.'

We watch as the man slowly saunters to the door. He starts speaking to the cops in an amiable sort of way. After a moment, though, we start to hear him using words like equal rights and freedom of passage. Everyone in the diner turns to watch the altercation as he raises his voice. After a minute, he's shaking with anger and pointing at the police in a threatening way.

In the next instant he clutches his chest and grabs both the cops. It looks like he's having a heart attack.

'Come on,' Brodie says. 'Now's our chance.'

I'm so entranced by the stranger's performance that I'd forgotten it was all simply an act to create a diversion. I don't know what his profession is, but he should consider acting. As the crowd assembles around the man who has now fallen to the floor with the cops trying to revive him, Brodie leads us around the counter and into the kitchen. A black haired woman is standing at a bench cutting up tomatoes. She looks at us curiously and says something to us in Spanish.

I have no idea what she is trying to communicate so I simply smile and point to the back door. We keep moving. A moment later we're in a back alley behind the diner. Just as we start away from the eatery, a voice yells from behind us.

Two cops hurry down the alley towards us.

Obviously they were patrolling the area and saw our escape.

'You kids were on that train, weren't you?' one of them says.

I look confused. 'What train?'

His partner frowns. 'I think we'd better have a little talk to you.'

Dan frowns at them. 'You don't need to talk to us.'

Both the men look at him. For a long moment it's as if time has come to a halt. They stare at him, mesmerized. Finally one of them nods in agreement.

'That's right,' he says dully. 'We don't need to speak to you.'

'We weren't on the train,' Dan says.

'You weren't on the train,' the other cop says.

My mouth drops open. I can't believe what I'm seeing. Dan is somehow brainwashing the cops into following his instructions. Obviously this is another little aspect to his powers he has forgotten to mention to us.

Of course, what's that thing they say about the

corruption of power?

'We're not the droids you're looking for.' Dan is now in full swing. He's smiling broadly now and gives us a big wink.

'Star Wars?' I murmur. 'You're giving us Star Wars?'

'They're not the droids we're looking for,' the cop says, although even he seems puzzled by what he's saying.

'May the force be with you,' Dan says gravely. 'Always.'

The cops nod, turn and head back down the lane in the opposite direction. At the end they turn and disappear from sight. Brodie and I look to each other and then to Dan.

Brodie grabs his arm. 'You can control minds?'

'Did it occur to you to mention this?' I ask.

'I was about to,' he says. 'But I didn't get a chance.'

Brodie looks furious. 'Don't you ever try this on me!'

Dan holds up his hands. 'I promise I will never do anything to you guys. Ever.'

He seems sincere, I think, though I can understand Brodie's anger. It's a horrible idea to think of someone manipulating you against your will. Someone taking away your free will and using you like a puppet.

'So where do we go from here?' I ask.

Dan's smiles. 'Wherever you want.'

Chapter Eleven

The view is fantastic. Even I have to admit it. But that's not too surprising. We have just rented the entire penthouse suite of The Robison, a hotel on Madison Avenue. It's not the best hotel in town, but it's close to it. Certainly beats living on the streets.

The more I think about the image in my mind of the wheat field, the more I decide I'm not from New York. I don't know how I came to be here, but somehow a boy living in a rural farming area got hijacked and dropped off in one of the world's biggest cities.

At least I'm not roughing it anymore. The penthouse of The Robison is as good as luxury gets. It has six bedrooms and an open plan living area with leather lounges and television in every room, including the bathroom. Not that the television is worth watching. It's the same old thing. Wars. Fears of financial recession. A feel good story about a dog rescued from a well in Siberia.

The leasing of the place came easy, though I

can't say I felt relaxed during any part of it. We simply went up to the front desk and Dan asked for the best apartment in the building. For a few seconds the man looked down his nose at him. Then Dan produced a wallet full of imaginary money and handed him a wad of it.

Later they'll check their takings and find they're down by several thousand dollars. Okay, I don't feel right about it. Neither does Brodie, but it's better than spending another night in the warehouse. Ultimately it's a question of survival.

Well, this is surviving, alright.

Room service has already delivered pizzas, chips and soft drinks three times. That's after we'd already cleaned out the contents of the mini bar. Dan suggested sampling the extensive range of alcohol available to us, but I vetoed it. We need to be clear headed in case guys with guns come knocking at the door.

Of course, Brodie and Dan are both super powered. One of Dan's additional abilities seems to be able to multi-process eating pizza, drinking coke and playing a computer game called Planet of Hell while lounging sideways on a sofa.

Oh, as well as carrying on a conversation.

'Is this the life, or is this the life?' he asks.

'This is the life,' I agree.

'But is it ethical?' Brodie asks.

'What does that mean?' Dan frowns, killing a demon and taking another quick bite of pizza.

'Ethical. Moral. The right thing to do.' She looked pissed about the whole thing. 'Aren't we supposed to be using our powers for good?'

'No-one gave me an instruction manual.' Dan looks at me. 'How about you?'

'No.' Although I'm not actually in the super hero club, so I probably shouldn't be saying anything. 'I don't think there's anything wrong with doing this for a couple of days. Then we can look at our options.'

'Which are?' Brodie asks.

I sigh. That's a good question to which I don't have a good answer. I'm not really sure where we go from here. We tried going back to the office of

Cygnus Industries and found nothing there. Brodie has had an image in her head of city surrounding a harbor, but unfortunately half the cities in the world seem to be located next to harbors. She might be referring to Sydney. She even has a memory of the Sydney Harbor Bridge, but she may have picked that up from a tourist brochure.

We seem to have hit a dead end.

I pull out the notebook again and leaf through the pages randomly.

'What's that?' Dan asks.

I explain to him about the book and he asks to have a look at it. For a long time he examines the pages closely without comment. Then he checks out the spine. His eyes narrow.

'I think there's something built into the spine,' he says.

I take the book from him. It takes me a moment to realize he's right. The spine is quite thick. A lot thicker than any regular hardcover book. It's hard to believe I didn't notice it before.

'Get me a knife,' I say.

A moment later I'm cutting carefully along the edge of the book. An object slips out into my hand. I've never seen anything like it. It looks vaguely like a flash drive for a computer, but it's much thinner. When I hold it up to the light it gets even stranger. The interior is sparkling, but it's like looking at a precious stone like an opal. It flashes with shades of red and yellow and green.

The others examine it too, but none of us can agree to its purpose.

Brodie thinks it's a piece of high tech gadgetry. Dan posits that it's a gem stone that's fallen out of its housing. I simply have no idea. I search my memory for several more seconds, but nothing comes to mind. At that moment room service arrives with more pizza, so I put the object into my pocket and decide to give it more thought later.

We sit and eat and watch an episode of The Simpsons. It's a rerun. Everything on the television seems to be reruns and old movies. I wander out onto the balcony where day has begun to give way to evening. Clouds have swallowed the sky again. I haven't seen the stars since, well, I don't know when. As the sky darkens, the city lights slowly come to life. It's a beautiful sight.

After a while I begin to think about Brodie and Dan's powers. It seems strange they have inherited abilities, but I don't seem to be any different to any other person. Looking down at my hands, I point them at planter boxes and vases.

Rise, I command.

Nothing happens.

I hear something stifling a laugh behind me.

Brodie.

'Laugh all you want,' I tell her. 'I will have my revenge.'

'Good luck with that.'

We both lean on the railing and look out at the city. She is so close her arm is almost touching mine. I get the irrational sense that I want to touch her hand, but I know it would freak her out. Instead, I give her a smile. She doesn't disappoint me. She smiles back.

'Aarrgh.'

The voice comes from behind us.

Dan.

He stumbles onto the balcony as if in pain. He has his hands clasped tightly over his ears as if trying to shut out a loud noise.

'What is it?' I ask.

He looks at us fearfully. 'I can hear voices,' he says. 'Two people. Kids like us. They're screaming.'

Brodie and I exchange glances.

'They're screaming,' I echo dumbly.

He nods. 'Yes,' Dan says. 'They're being tortured by that man Ravana.'

Chapter Twelve

My blood runs cold at the news.

Ravana.

The memories of my time in the room come flooding back. For a few hours I have driven him from my mind. Now that I think about it, I wonder how I could have so successfully avoided thinking about him. It must be my mind shielding me from the pain of the experience. The truth of it is that I will never forget that monster. He will be a part of me for as long as I live.

'How can you know this?' Brodie asks.

Dan shakes his head. 'I have no idea. The feeling comes and goes. One second I'm here and then I'm in their heads. Ravana is applying that…probe to their hands. It's a girl and a guy.'

The probe. The thought of it makes me want to throw up.

Still, we need to help them. If we can.

'Do you know where they're being kept?' Brodie asks.

Dan focuses for a minute. He looks out across the city. 'I'm not sure. I get a feeling the building is over in that direction.' He points to the east. 'I think we need to go that way.'

Fortunately we've got a car. It's a late model convertible. Again, thanks to Dan, we were able to purchase one for an apple and a copy of the daily paper. Mind you, I think the man thought he was collecting about twenty thousand in cold, hard cash, but he seemed happy with the deal anyway.

Brodie and I are in the front seat. I drive while Dan focuses on trying to find the building. It's like driving around with a human metal detector. We spend half an hour with Dan saying things like, 'it's getting warmer' and 'no, now we're moving away'. At the end of it I think all we've done is driven around in circles and used up half a tank of petrol.

Finally I pull over.

'I think you need to focus,' I tell Dan.

'I'm trying.'

Brodie makes a suggestion. 'What if you were to move out of the minds of the kids in the building?

Can you do that?'

Dan considers this. 'I can try.'

'Maybe you can latch onto someone else's mind,' Brodie says. 'Someone who's leaving the building.'

Dan takes a deep breath, closes his eyes and focuses. For a few minutes he says nothing. I glance out the window and notice people walking past the vehicle. One glances in. Obviously this must look a little weird; two people staring at a guy with his eyes shut. After a while Dan clears his throat.

'I'm with someone in the elevator. It's a guy. He doesn't know Ravana or his organization. He just works somewhere in the building. The elevator is coming to a halt. It's at ground level. He's getting out. Leaving the building. I can look back. I can see…'

Dan's eyes open wide. 'I can see it. I can see the building. It's…'

The moment seems to last forever.

Then he tells us the address of a building on East Seventy-First Street.

Brodie shakes her head in amazement. 'You're incredible.'

Dan wipes sweat from his brow. 'I know.'

'Modest too,' I lean over the seat and hit Dan on the shoulder.

I start the car and angle it into the traffic. It doesn't take long for us to arrive at the address. It's a tall, modern looking office block surrounded by similar buildings. It's hard to believe there are two kids being tortured in such a location.

The thought turns my stomach.

We climb out of the car. For the first time, I'm feeling kind of nervous. I feel like I'm the spare wheel in this organization. It looks like Brodie can single-handedly fight an army to a standstill. Dan can move objects with the power of his mind and get into people's heads. I can—

Well, I know how to drive. Maybe I can be like Alfred the butler in the Batman comics and drive the others places and make cocoa at appropriate times.

We stop in front of the building.

'I know this is probably too much to expect,' I say, turning to Dan. 'But any idea which floor Ravana is on?'

Dan shakes his head. 'No. We might just have to wing it from here.'

We enter the main lobby. Adjacent to the elevators is a chart of the building occupants. There are a lot of them. We spend the next few minutes perusing the list. Finally we turn to each other in frustration.

'Nothing stands out,' Brodie shakes her head. 'Why can't bad guys identify themselves as such?'

'You mean, like Evil Inc?' Dan asks.

'Yeah,' I say, staring at the list. 'Or Bad For U?'

At that moment a guy enters the lobby and passes us without a glance. He disappears into an elevator. Dan has been watching him from the corner of his eye. He leans close to us as the elevator departs.

'I picked up something from him,' Dan says.

'The flu?' I ask.

'I couldn't get a clear picture, but it was a negative vibe.'

We wander over to the elevator and watch the changing display. It stops at the twenty-fifth floor. The directory lists them as Stanley Imports. I glance at the others.

'What do you think?'

Brodie shrugs. 'We've got nothing to lose. Let's do it.'

It seems strange standing patiently in the ascending elevator. I don't know about the others, but my throat has gone dry. My heart is beating like crazy. I look at Brodie and a sweat has broken out on her brow. Only Dan seems completely confident.

It's because he's younger than us, I think.

A chill runs down my spine. How old is Dan? Maybe fifteen. Brodie and I aren't much older. We're a bunch of teenagers about to launch an attack on Ravana and his cronies and *we don't have a plan.*

The idea makes me dizzy. *We haven't prepared for this.* We're marching blindly into this place with no clue as to what we're about to do when we reach the floor or where to go when we get there. *It's absolutely insane.* I open my mouth to speak, but as I do the elevator draws to a halt.

The doors slide open.

I think we're walking into hell.

Chapter Thirteen

The first thing we see is a big empty semi-circular room. A reception desk is set back about twenty feet from the elevator. Beige carpet covers the floor. Behind the desk there's an empty chair and partition walls. The words Stanley Imports are positioned at eye level in an italicized font. No-one is in sight.

The only other object I can see is a potted plant to the right of the elevator doors.

Brodie and Dan step out and stride straight into the heart of the reception area. Instead of following them, I place myself between the two elevator doors to stop them from closing. While the sensors register a blockage, the doors will not close.

I hope.

My stomach is bouncing around like it's full of jelly. There's something bad here. I can't put my finger on it, but something doesn't make sense. It's something about the furniture…

Brodie stops in the middle of the reception

area. She looks around for a door. Dan strides straight to the reception desk. He looks like he's ready to pick up pieces of furniture with his mind and start hurling them around.

The elevator doors want to close. The door behind me jars against my back and then slides back into the recess. Brodie turns at the sound and looks curiously at me. Then her eyes shift as she surveys the semi-circular chamber again. Her eyes narrow. Her mouth settles into a frown.

'Where are these turkeys?' Dan asks. 'They're afraid to take us on.'

He turns around and for the first time looks a little unsure of himself. It's hard to show bravado when there's no-one to display it to. The door of the elevator tries to close again. There's probably someone on the fiftieth floor looking at their watch and wondering who's holding them up.

Let them wait.

'There's something wrong here,' I tell them.

Brodie looks at me worriedly. 'I think you're right.'

Leaning out into the foyer, I'm just about to tell them to get back into the elevator when I catch movement in two directions at once. Two slots open up in opposing walls. A machine gun appears in both.

Dan looks confused. Brodie takes a single step towards the elevator.

The guns open fire.

One second there is silence. The next there is an explosion of sound that makes your eardrums hurt. I throw my arms out, screaming, but my words are drowned by the explosion of the guns. Both Brodie and Dan are caught between the two weapons. They throw themselves to the ground, but I immediately see bullets slamming into carpet, ricocheting off the ceiling, cutting the reception desk to pieces, slamming into the opposing walls.

It should be a bloodbath, but somehow they start crawling towards the elevator. A bullet ricochets past my ear and smashes the mirror behind me. Pieces of carpet are flying into the air. Plaster is reduced to dust. There's so much debris flying around it's almost impossible to see the far wall.

Brodie gets to the elevator first. She reaches back for Dan and drags him in after her. Only then does my focus turn away from the arena of destruction. I slam the button for the ground floor. Even as I do, I wonder if Ravana and his men have some special control over the elevator that will stop it from moving.

If they do, it's game over.

It seems to take an eternity, but to my enormous relief the doors slide shut and the sound of gunfire dulls to silence. After another unbearably long second, the elevator starts to descend.

Brodie looks up at me. Her face is stricken with disbelief.

She tries to speak. 'It was…it was…'

'A trap,' I say.

Dan is lying on the floor in fetal position. Shaking. I kneel next to him and search for blood. I don't find any.

'Dan?' He's looking straight at my knee. There's drool around his mouth. 'Dan? Can you hear me?'

'He's in shock,' Brodie says.

So is she. Her hair is everywhere. She's not pale. She's white. A color so like ivory that it looks like she's had her skin dyed.

'Are you hit?' I ask her.

'No.' She shakes her head. 'Get him on his feet. We've got to get out of here.'

I nod. Somehow I physically lift Dan from the ground. I get one of his arms around my shoulders. He looks as pale as Brodie. I wipe the spittle from his mouth and get Brodie to check him again. There's no blood. Somehow both of them escaped without a scratch.

Dan might be a mess now, but at least he came through when the going got tough.

When the elevator doors open, Dan's legs start working of their own accord. Obviously his conscious mind is not working, but the automatic functions—breathing, circulation, walking—are still operational.

The only evidence in the elevator that anything happened is the broken mirror at the back. Apart from that, there's no evidence someone just tried to cut us to pieces in a hail of gunfire. Possibly Ravana and his cronies have their entire floor soundproofed. That's the only explanation for why dozens of police aren't pouring into the building. The racket upstairs was so loud it just made the Gunfight at the OK Corral look like a shooting gallery at the fair.

We cross the lobby. A business man, obviously heading back to the office to pick up some forgotten paperwork, gives us a curious glance, but I glare at him and he passes without comment.

We escape the building. By that point I'm able to grab Dan's shoulder and drag him along as we jog down the sidewalk to the car. My hands are still shaking by the time I climb behind the wheel, but there's no way I can expect Brodie to drive. Despite her apparent calm, she's still obviously a mess.

'It was the furniture,' I tell them as we pull into the traffic.

'What was?' Brodie asks.

'I had a strange feeling about that reception area. There was nowhere for anyone to sit. I didn't realize it at the time…'

My voice trails away to nothing. It's not important now. I keep checking the rear view mirror to see if anyone's following. If they are, they're good, because I can't see them.

Dan's in the back seat. Up till now he's been sitting up with his eyes staring into nothing. Now I notice he looks incredibly tired. He's struggling to keep his eyes open. Must be the delayed shock. Sleep is the best thing for him. For all of us.

'Things got pretty hairy back there,' I tell him as I weave around a truck. 'But you came through, Dan.' I feel I need to bolster his spirits after the aborted attempt. 'You really saved our skins.'

Dan shakes his head. 'No. No, that wasn't me.'

'What do you mean?' I ask him. 'You saved the day back there.'

'No I didn't,' he says quietly. 'I was a mess. There were bullets flying everywhere. I couldn't do a thing. Couldn't focus. Couldn't even think.' He shakes his head again. 'I didn't do anything.'

'Well,' says Brodie. 'If it wasn't me and it wasn't Dan…'

I know both of them are looking at me. I don't know what to say. Up till now I haven't displayed any abilities. Nothing at all. Now I think back to the hail of gunfire back at the building. It was a turkey shoot. Somebody saved them from certain death.

Was it me?

Chapter Fourteen

It's a beautiful day in the park. The sun is warm on our shoulders. A breeze is gently shaking the trees. There are clouds in the sky, but there's no chance of rain. People are flying kites. Kids are playing with their dog. Someone is marching a pram around a lake. A couple holds hands on a park bench.

We're here for entirely different reasons.

We're here to see if I have super powers.

Roughly twelve hours have passed since our aborted rescue of the kids in Ravana's tower. Dan climbed out of bed embarrassed though grateful to be alive. Brodie looked a little stressed, but also determined. She took charge and ordered breakfast from room service for the three of us. We all ate like starving people and finished our meals in silence. Finally Brodie told us to shower because we had a lot of work to do.

'Like what?' Dan asked.

'We're taking a drive to the country,' Brodie says. 'We're going to test Axel's powers.'

'What powers would they be?' I ask cautiously.

'That's what we're going to find out,' she replied.

So three hours later we're not in the country, but we are in a large parkland area on the outskirts of the city. We wander through the park until we find a secluded corner surrounded by trees. A rock in the middle seems to be the perfect target upon which to practice. We sit around the rock in a circle.

'We'll start with you trying to move the rock,' Brodie says. 'Now, just focus on it. Get a sense of its size and weight and dimensions.'

'Okay,' I say after a moment.

'Now try to lift it.'

I stare at the rock intently, willing it to rise up off the ground. I imagine myself under it, lifting it off the grass, making it rise into the air and making it soar high above the trees.

It does none of the above. It sits there like a rock.

I continue to stare at it.

'Really focus on it, Axel,' Dan says.

'I am.'

'Imagine you're surrounding the rock. Trying to lift it.'

'Yeah, I am.'

'You're making it rise—'

'That's what I'm trying to do—'

'Be the rock,' Dan urges, his eyes growing wide. 'Be the rock.'

'I am a rock,' I tell him. 'I'm lumpy and bored.' I shake my head in frustration. 'Nothing's happening. It won't move.'

'You need to concentrate on it longer,' Brodie says. 'Really get into it.'

'This doesn't make sense,' I tell them. 'Why do I need to focus now? Last night it looked like I could deflect bullets with ease.'

Neither of them have an answer.

'Maybe you need a smaller rock,' Dan suggests.

'Maybe.'

My eyes search the field for a smaller boulder,

but instead I find myself staring at the sky. I revise my earlier weather report. It could rain later. The wind has picked up in the trees. They are being tossed around more ferociously with every passing second. I decide to focus on one of the trees. Maybe if I can make the branches stop moving...

They stop.

It's an eerie sensation. All the other trees are still being tossed about by the breeze. The single tree I'm looking at is stationary. In fact, the longer I look at it the more I can see a cocoon, like a transparent bubble, encasing the branches.

I grab Brodie's arm.

'What is it?' she asks.

'The tree.' I point with a shaking hand. 'Look.'

Both she and Dan look at the still branches. After a moment, Dan says, 'How are you doing that?'

I let out a deep exhalation and realize I've been holding my breath. 'I don't know. I was looking at the branches and sort of willed them to stop moving.'

'And they did,' Brodie says.

I nod.

'Try lifting the stone now,' Dan says.

I give it another attempt, but still it won't move an inch. I even go over to it and lift it up with my hands to make certain it hasn't been cemented into the ground. No. It's just a plain ordinary rock.

Holding it in my hand, I focus on it until my head hurts.

Nothing.

Brodie has been watching me and frowning. Now she looks back at the moving trees and I see a determined expression cross her face.

'Axel,' she says. 'I've got an idea. Try the trees again, but this time make the branches move more instead of standing still.'

'That's right,' Dan says, nodding. 'You could be a new type of superhero. You might be Tree-man.'

'Tree-man?' I repeat.

I hope not.

Dropping the rock, I turn my attention to the trees again. This time I focus on trying to make the branches move even more. I'm not sure what's going to happen, but I'm on a roll now and I don't want to stop.

Holding out both arms, I give it all I've got.

And nothing happens.

'Okay,' I say. 'This is no fun.'

I stare impatiently at the trees, watching the branches move gently in the breeze. Slowly, an idea occurs to me.

This time I focus on the wind in the branches. The effect is instantaneous. It's as if there's a breeze coming from our direction, blowing the branches away from us; it's like the exhaust from a jet engine. Excitedly, I push even harder until I hear the sound of cracking boughs from the tree. Within seconds, branches are breaking loose and flying away out of sight.

'Holy cow,' Dan says.

'It's the air,' I tell them. 'I can control air.'

Now I turn back to the rock. This time I don't think about moving the rock. Instead I think about using the air to do all the work. The boulder trembles, shudders and starts to roll away from us. Finally I pretend to use it like a bowling ball and it bounces away from us at high speed and disappears into the bushes.

'That's amazing,' Brodie says. 'Air...' She starts thinking. 'Air is pretty powerful. Think of hurricanes and tornados. They can slam pieces of straw into timber like nails.'

'And knock down houses,' Dan says. 'Flatten towns.'

'And lift things,' I say. 'They can make things airborne. Carry things away.'

'You're not thinking...' Brodie's voice trails away to nothing.

I gather the air around and under me.

A moment later I'm flying.

Chapter Fifteen

Brodie and Dan stare at me in astonishment.

'That's awesome,' Dan says, his jaw dropping open. 'Do it to me! Make me fly too!'

'Hold on, hold on,' I reply. I'm about a foot off the ground and I'm already terrified. I remember that I don't like heights. Having nothing under your feet is a disconcerting sensation. I don't know how the astronauts handle it. There's no way I'm taking any passengers.

Not yet, anyway.

Looking down, I can see the same transparent bubble under me, lifting me up off the ground. Now I focus on making it lift me even higher. Within seconds I'm about six feet off the ground and rising.

'Pick up a rock,' I tell Brodie. 'And throw it at me.'

She picks up something about the size of a coin and hurls it at me. I form a shield and it bounces off and hits Dan on the head.

'Ouch!'

'Sorry.'

So that's how Brodie and Dan were kept safe when the guns opened fire. I formed some sort of solid wall of air between the bullets and them. The physics of it is beyond me, but even air can be compressed so tightly that it's impenetrable.

Air. Who would have thought it?

I'm Air Man.

Hmm, might work on the name.

The sensible thing now would be to descend from my lofty perch. Instead, I can't help but feel so elated by the experience that I want to keep going. My fear of heights seems to be evaporating by the second. I hear a sound from below and realize it's Brodie calling to me. She looks terrified.

'I'm okay,' I call back to her.

She yells something out, but I can't hear her.

Now I work on changing my direction. I imagine a bed next to me and then I try lying on it. Well, it seems like a great idea, but instead I find I'm leaning against a wall of air.

Okay, so then I imagine extending the

platform under me. I kneel down onto it and then lay down flat. Straight down beneath me I see Dan and Brodie staring up at me in astonishment. They're not half as surprised as I am. Or as frightened. I can feel the platform beneath me. I can even see it shimmering slightly. But I'm still floating in mid air. It's a strange combination of elation and terror.

I stick out an arm over my head.

Okay, it's corny, but it works for Superman.

I will myself forward. For a few seconds I think nothing's happening. Then I realize I'm slowly moving away from the clearing. I head towards a cloud. The wind tears at me as I fly higher. It gets colder by the second. Mist whirls around me. I should be concerned, but I'm momentarily beyond fear.

I'm flying.

Looking down, fear comes back with a vengeance. Actually I almost die of fright. I'm so far off the ground I can no longer see Brodie and Dan. The park is a maze of shapes. Green ovals. A pond. A river. The suburbs surrounding the city are a patchwork quilt. The city rises in the distance, a cathedral of steel and glass.

I fall.

It happens so suddenly that I'm not aware of it for a few seconds. Then I realize the bubble that has been supporting me has disintegrated into shards. I force my eyes shut. It's the last thing I feel like doing, but it helps me to focus. When I open my eyes again the platform has regained its integrity.

I decide to go higher. It's crazy because I don't know anything about my powers. I might run out of *oomph* a thousand feet up, but I don't care. My fear of heights has disappeared, replaced by an unhealthy confidence. As I zoom straight up, the air continues to get colder and thinner. There is a strong cross wind and I've got to say it isn't the pleasant experience I was expecting.

I veer towards the city.

It would be insanity to be seen. I can imagine the headlines. *Boy Spotted Flying Over City! Air force Shoots Down Flying Boy! Post-Mortem Reveals Drug Use!* Those sort of headlines, I don't need.

I'm determined to stay fairly high up. I'm still

hundreds of feet above the tallest buildings. I can see a number of helicopters cruising across town, but I stay well away from them. I have no intention of scaring any chopper pilots. The city below me is a complicated network of streets and unfamiliar landmarks. I don't recognize anything at all until I catch sight of the Hudson and the East River. They start to put things into perspective.

That's when I hit the blimp.

One second I'm focused on working out the relationship between the streets. In the next, I'm aware of an odd droning sound and a big silver wall cuts across in front of me. The helium filled balloon is advertising Toto's Donuts. I slam into it at an angle and the whole thing wobbles uncontrollably. Even its engine whirrs erratically.

Fortunately it's automated. No-one's in the gondola that hangs beneath, but the episode is enough to makes me realize I'm acting stupidly. These things are made for people to see from ground level and I've positioned myself right next to it.

Real clever.

I zoom up higher again and follow a main arterial road out of the city. More out of luck than design I locate the park and start to descend. Once again, I find it incredibly difficult to orientate myself. Finally I see our little clearing. Dan and Brodie have taken refuge under a tree.

I'd like to say that I gracefully descended like a God from the heavens, but that would be a lie. Actually I come in too fast at too steep an angle and I land sideways, my legs skimming along the ground for several feet. Finally the rest of my body hits the grass and I roll over several times to disperse my momentum.

Brodie and Dan race over to me. To their credit, they don't give me a hard time about the landing. They're impressed I can do the flying thing at all. They help me to my feet and brush me off.

'You should have seen Dan after you took off,' Brodie laughs. 'He thought he might have a latent flying ability. He kept on leaping up and down like a jumping bean.'

'Did you get anywhere?' I ask him.

'Naaa,' he shakes his head. 'I'm earthbound.'

I glance at Brodie.

'I'm a landlubber too,' she says. 'But something did happen while you were away.'

'What?'

'I had those voices in my head again,' Dan says. He actually looks a little sick at the thought. 'They were screaming again.'

'They're being tortured,' Brodie says. 'Somehow, we've got to save them.'

I hold up a hand. 'I've got a plan.' On the way back down to the ground I noticed the weather was changing. Good. It will work in our favor. 'We're going back to Ravana's building, but this time we'll be prepared.'

Chapter Sixteen

By the time we're in position, the weather has disintegrated. And in a big way. Driving back into town, storm clouds swept over the city. The radio station warned there was rain on the way. Even a chance of hail.

All the better.

We're standing on the roof of the Lexor Building. It's just another skyscraper in the heart of Manhattan, but it's important to us because it's right across the road from Ravana's building.

Everything has worked according to plan, although there are a couple of things we didn't take into account. Thanks to Dan, the electrical substation that controls this side of town is out of commission. He was able to project a piece of metal into the heart of the thing, knocking out power to an eight block city grid.

We were pleased with our efforts until we realized we still needed to get to the roof of the Lexor Building without elevators. This meant walking up thirty flights of stairs.

Even for young, fit teenagers such as ourselves, it was a struggle. By the time we reached the roof, our legs were jelly.

'Are you sure you couldn't just fly us up here?' Dan asks.

I shake my head. 'I want to keep that to a minimum. The less chance that people have of seeing me, the better.'

This is an era where anyone with a cell phone is a journalist. I want to stay off YouTube for as long as possible.

There's only about fifty feet between us and the other building. Back in the park, I practiced lifting Dan and Brodie into the air and landing again. While I wouldn't carry both of them at the same time, I found I was able to master keeping two of us in flight at the same time. I hang onto the other person and extend the flying platform under both of us. It's not elegant. I don't have the Superman technique handled yet, but it works.

It starts to rain, a driving torrential downpour

driven by high winds. In one way it's a nuisance, but at least it creates another diversion and we need all the help we can get. First I fly Brodie across to the other building. It's windy, but we make it across without incident. By the time I return to take Dan, the winds seem to have doubled. The only way we make it is that I stay completely focused on the task at hand. Our landing is a little rough, but it's one we can live with.

'Dan, we need the door open,' I tell him.

'Gotcha,' he replies.

It takes him longer than expected. The driving wind and rain don't help things. Finally the lock breaks and the door swings loose in the wind. We hurry in from the rain and find ourselves in a darkened stairwell. The only lighting is an emergency exit sign above the door; it must be operated either by a generator or stored solar power.

'I don't hear an alarm,' Brodie says.

'Let's hope there isn't one,' I say.

We make our way down the stairs. Fortunately the doors are marked with the floor number in large letters. We listen closely at the fire door leading to the twenty-fifth floor. Silence. That doesn't mean there isn't a guard at the door. There could be ten guys on the other side waiting for us.

We just have to take our chances. Dan focuses on forcing the lock open. He does it as quietly as possible, but it sounds like a train wreck in the silence of the stairwell. Every cracking of the metal is magnified tenfold.

Finally, Brodie eases it open and checks in both directions. She waves us in after her. From here, we don't really have a plan except Dan has been able to give us a general idea of where he thinks the other teenagers are being held. It's on the other side of the building, so our intention is to get there without being seen.

We go down the corridor and turn left into another passageway. We're halfway down it when two guys come through a doorway. At first we're lucky. They turn immediately away from us, but at the last instant one of them must have spotted us from the corner of his eye. He stops and starts to turn.

That's enough to get Brodie moving.

Man. Is she fast or is she fast?

In about two seconds she's covered the distance between us and them and she's knocked one guy's head against the other. It's like something out of The Three Stooges. They go down in an untidy pile with barely a sound. Both men are security guards armed with guns, batons and mace. We drag them into the room they exited. It's some sort of meeting area. Hopefully they won't wake up anytime soon.

We continue down the corridor. After a moment, Dan grabs our arms and drags us to a halt.

'I can feel them.' He rubs the side of his head. 'They're close. And in pain.'

I think again of Ravana's device and I feel the hatred bubbling up inside me. I push the emotion to one side. Later there will be time to dwell on him. Now we need to focus on the task at hand.

We reach another corridor. Brodie peers around the corner. There is the sound of a door closing followed by receding footsteps. She waits until the footsteps have gone silent before she turns to us.

'I got a glimpse of the room those guys left,' she says. 'It's some sort of guard room. There's about a dozen guys in there. If we can trap them in there…'

She looks at Dan.

'Consider it done,' he says. 'They don't call me Metal Boy for nothing.'

Personally, I'm unaware that anyone has ever called him Metal Boy, but I let it pass.

Seconds later we're hurrying past the door. Dan has somehow melted the lock together. Just as we turn into the next corridor we hear someone trying to exit the room. There's the sound of a commotion.

'We need to hurry,' Brodie says.

We turn another corner. This time our luck goes south because there's two security guards heading straight towards us. We adopt a maneuver we talked about in the car heading over here.

I throw up a shield as the guys pull out their guns. They start firing, but the bullets bounce off and ricochet into the side walls. Dan focuses on their weapons. As we advance towards them I can see the barrels of their guns bending back on themselves. One of the guys doesn't notice his gun has turned into a pretzel. It blows up in his hand. At the same time I drop the barrier and Brodie moves in on them.

All of five seconds later we're stepping over their unconscious bodies.

'Remind me never to argue with you,' I tell her.

She flashes a smile at me and we keep moving.

We've lost the advantage of surprise, but that becomes a mute point because the next corner we come around has a heavily fortified metal door at the end of the corridor.

'We've got to move!' I yell. 'Dan...uh, Metal Boy!'

I hear Dan grunt with effort and the door flies off the hinges away from us. Beyond it we see a line of guys protecting another door. They open fire immediately, but by now I've got my shield up. Bullets are flying everywhere. There are six of them with guns versus the three of us who are completely unarmed.

They don't stand a chance.

One of the guys suddenly drops to the ground or I should say he is *dragged* to the ground by his own weapon. There's no telling what he thinks of his gun operating of its own accord, but within seconds it has trained itself on the feet of his companions. It opens fire and takes out the lower limbs of the other men. They hit the floor, crying out in pain and writhing in agony. My stomach rolls over at the sight. I don't like to see anyone in pain, but they happened to pick the wrong side. Dan bends the barrels of the other guns, then turns his attention to the entrance. It's another metal door and it takes him a few seconds to break it out of its frame.

It hits the ground with a crash.

We can see another chamber inside the room. Some sort of cell where two people are waiting expectantly. A girl and a guy. They have similar features. Probably brother and sister. As I step forward to enter the room, a figure with a gun suddenly appears.

Ravana.

The gun in his hand is aimed directly at my chest. Just as he fires I realize Brodie has moved like lightning and already pushed me to one side.

She's still not fast enough.

I still feel the agony of the impact as the bullet slams into me.

Chapter Seventeen

One minute I'm on my feet. The next I'm on the ground. Brodie takes out Ravana with one punch. So intent was he on shooting the first person he saw beyond the doorway that he didn't even notice her or Dan.

I'm on the floor, but I don't know what has hurt more. The bullet wound or Brodie's shove. It was like being hit by a truck. Grabbing my side, I struggle to my feet. I'm bleeding, but I'm alive. It's only a flesh wound. Brodie has saved my life.

I want to thank her, but we're running out of time. We're surrounded by a pile of wounded men. There could be more guards on the way. Plus Ravana is recovering quickly. He's motionless on the floor, but his eyes are beginning to flutter.

The teenagers on the other side of the glass are pointing at the door. Dan focuses on the door. It groans within its housing, but doesn't move. After a few seconds he looks at me in despair.

'It's too big,' he says. 'I can't move it.'

'Stand back,' I tell Brodie and Dan.

They wave the teens away from the glass. It's obviously a number of inches thick. Obviously Ravana was determined to keep them at bay. I imagine an invisible spear. It only takes a few seconds before I can see it clearly in the air. Drawing it back I force all my will into throwing it at the glass.

Nothing happens.

'Oh hell,' I say in dismay.

Brodie laughs and grabs something off Ravana's waist. It's a set of keys.

'It's all break and smash with you boys,' she says cheekily. 'Isn't it?'

She opens the door using the second key on the chain. The boy and the girl exit the cell. The guy grabs my shoulder.

'Who are you people?' he asks. 'What's going on?'

'Later,' I tell him. 'Just tell us your names.'

'I'm Chad,' he introduces himself. 'And this girl is Ebony. I think she's my sister. I know that sounds weird, but—'

'Don't worry about it,' I wave him off. 'Weird is our version of normal.'

I immediately notice Chad has a slight accent. European. It's impossible to determine his origin.

Chad's eyes shift to Ravana. The sadist is fully awake now and staring at us fearfully. Absolute terror fills his eyes as he sees the expression on Chad's face.

'No...please...I was under orders!'

'You want mercy?' Chad asks incredulously. 'After hurting us with that implement for days? You want mercy?'

He draws back his fist. I'm not sure if he has some amazing power—which he probably does—or if he just intends to pummel Ravana. Either way, we don't have the time to deal with it. Ebony grabs his arm.

'Don't,' she says. Her voice is soft. She seems so frail. I can't help but wonder if Ravana has harmed more than her body over the last few days. 'He's a monster, but killing is wrong.'

Chad looks like he wants to argue, but he bites

his tongue. Thankfully Brodie is already heading through the first security door.

'Come on!' she says impatiently. 'Axel, I need you up here.'

I take up my position and throw a barrier around us. This is going to take more concentration than before. I'm trying to protect us both front and rear. Dan is first. Me second. Then Chad and Ebony and finally Brodie. Ebony seems dazed and unable to make sense of what's going on.

'We'll need your help,' Chad says to her.

She nods. 'What do we need?'

'Carbon,' he says.

I have no idea what they're talking about. We head down a corridor. By the time we've reached the end we can hear the sound of footsteps from behind us.

'There are more guards coming!' I tell Brodie.

'It's okay,' Chad says. 'Ebony.'

She nods. Then she kneels down and touches the carpeted floor behind us. It takes about three seconds for it to turn from beige carpet to black.

'What the hell?' I start.

'Keep moving,' Chad urges. He points at the carpet and then a trail of fire leaps from his fingers and hits the floor. What used to be carpet bursts into flames. Guards appear at the other end, but they're driven back by the flames. At the same time, the sprinkler system activates and water starts pouring from the ceiling.

Still, it's going to take a while to put out the fire.

More by luck than intention, we find the exit door and start up the stairs. The alarm system has activated and people are heading down the stairs to evacuate. Some of them look curiously at us as we head towards the roof, but no-one stops to question us.

We push the door open and seconds later we're outside. It's still raining. Now we've just got to get across to the other building and this whole ordeal will be over. I need to ferry everyone across. I take Ebony across and then Dan.

By the time I get back for Chad and Brodie, I

notice the pain in my side is worse. My shirt is stained with blood and the wound is stinging as if it's on fire. As I land, I see the door burst open from the fire escape. Two of Ravana's men appear in the doorway. Chad holds out a hand and suddenly they are both enveloped in flame.

'No!' I cry.

Both the guards disappear from sight.

'Why stop me?' Chad snaps. 'They would kill us without a thought!'

'Because it's wrong!' I draw back a fist. 'There'll be no killing while I'm here!'

'Don't touch me, you—'

Then Brodie is between us. 'This is no time for testosterone wars! We've got to get out of here.'

She's right. Of course. But I can't take both of them at once. I don't dare. The pain in my side is so bad I'm feeling sick.

I give them the bad news.

'Take Chad first,' Brodie tells me. 'After Chad's little fire display it'll be a while before anyone else comes up.'

'Okay.'

I grab him by the arm and within seconds we're zooming between the two buildings. I'm really not feeling well by now. Our landing is anything, but graceful. By the time I'm heading back for Brodie the opposite building is reverberating like it's splitting into two.

Landing, I grab Brodie by the arm and drag her over to the edge. The street is filled with fire brigade and police. It looks like the whole city is falling to pieces at the seams. I give myself a couple of seconds to focus.

That's it, I think. *Just form the platform. Make it strong.*

We start between the buildings. I dare not look down; my stomach is swishing about uncomfortably already. I might be sick at any moment. The bang of a door diverts my attention. I glance back to see Ravana on the other side. A bolt of flame hurls past my vision aimed directly at the madman.

At the same time I see Ravana has a weapon in his hand. It's not a normal gun. It's about three times the size. He pulls the trigger just as the flame hits him. A second later he is engulfed by fire.

A beam of light from the weapon hits us. The effect is instantaneous. I'm still focused on the invisible platform beneath my feet, but it evaporates into nothing. I see the expression of horror on Brodie's face.

I want to explain to Brodie, but there's no time. Whatever was in that beam *just wiped out my powers.*

We begin to fall.

Chapter Eighteen

They are the worst few seconds of my life, or the life I can remember, anyway. All I can think as we fall is that *we're going to die*. There's no surviving this. We're not invincible. We're just two teenagers who used to be super powered.

Now we're just two teenagers with seconds to live.

Until we hit the bridge. We hit the surface of it hard, but you won't hear any complaints from me. I want to scream with delight. We only fall about six feet before the bridge made of ice forms between the two buildings. I see Chad standing at the edge of the building, a grin breaking across his face.

Fire and ice. Those are his powers.

Fire and ice.

We climb up the ice bridge to join them on the roof. They help us over the edge. Dan is beside himself with excitement. He's jumping around like a dog. Chad looks exceptionally pleased with himself. Ebony still has not said a word. She's hiding behind a hand held nervously over her mouth.

'That's good work,' I tell Chad. 'Thanks.'

'Yeah,' he says. 'I know. I saved your ass. You owe me one.'

'I owe you?' Now is not the time to remind him about which one of us, until recently, was trapped in a cell. 'We need to get out of here, but first we have to get rid of that bridge.'

'I know,' he says.

He leans over the roof and points at the bridge. This time fire doesn't erupt from his hands. It's more of an intense heat that hits the ice bridge and melts it instantaneously. No-one on the street below will even notice the warmer water in the middle of this storm.

We make our way to the car. Fortunately I'm wearing a dark jacket which hides the bloody patch in my side. I'm feeling sick to the stomach. Chad offers to drive, but I forcefully tell him to climb in the back seat. Maybe I'm too harsh with him, but I'm fading fast now.

Brodie climbs behind the wheel and we zigzag

through the city back to the hotel. I'm asleep by the time we arrive. The others wake me up to assist me through the lobby of the hotel. They tell the desk clerk I've had too much to drink and he believes them. I'm barely able to walk by the time we reach our floor. Sometime later I wake up to hear Chad and Brodie arguing.

'—should be in a hospital,' Brodie is saying.

'That would only draw attention to us,' Chad says. 'That's the last thing—'

I pass out.

When I wake up again I realize I'm not wearing a shirt and Ebony is at my side. None of it makes any sense. Then I see she has a needle and thread in her hand.

I try to fight her off, but suddenly Brodie is holding me down. I don't resist. I don't fight. I trust Brodie.

Darkness comes again.

Sun is shining on my face when I wake up next. My entire body hurts like hell, but I roll out of bed and somehow land on my feet. Chad is at my side. He slaps my shoulder.

'How're you feeling, old man?' he asks.

He still has a cheeky expression on his face. God, I hate him. Was he born with this expression?

'I feel great,' I tell him. 'Really great.'

'This is a fantastic set up you guys have got,' he says, ignoring my sarcasm. 'Penthouse apartment. Room service. Views of the city.' He gives a whistle. 'Talk about living in the lap of luxury.'

I can't think too much about luxury now. The woozy, sick feel from the previous day is gone, but the pain in my side is so bad I'm thinking maybe hospital wasn't such a bad idea.

'I'm glad you like it,' I say. 'Who stitched me up?'

'Ebony,' he says. 'She's my sister. I think.'

'She probably is. She looks like you.'

'I think we're Norwegian,' Chad says. 'We can both remember fjords.'

'What are they?'

'Bodies of deep water surrounded by steep hills,' he explains. 'And we can speak four languages.

Norwegian, German, French and English.'

'That's a pretty strange superpower.'

He looks at me strangely. 'That's not a superpower. Most people in Europe speak several languages.' Plopping himself into a chair opposite the bed, he continues, 'You missed our bio last night, so let me fill you in.'

Both Chad and Ebony found themselves lying on the beach a few miles out of the city. Like us, they had no idea as to their identities until they checked their clothing. They quickly assumed they were brother and sister. Completely by accident, they realized they had powers. Chad was feeling cold and wanted to make a fire.

He accidentally set a local boat shed alight. He then just as quickly put it out with a shower of snow. It took Ebony a little longer to work out her ability. She ended up assuming she didn't have one until she realized she was thirsty and wanted a glass of water.

'We were sitting on a park bench at the time,' Chad recalls. 'Then we were sitting in a puddle of water.'

They realized Ebony was able to transmute objects from one substance to another. Once they realized they had their powers, they decided not to go to the police. Chad was concerned they might be thrown into a lab and used for experiments.

As luck would have it, that almost happened anyway.

They were living in an abandoned factory when Ravana's men attacked them. Chad tried to fight them off, but they were hit with that device that robbed them of their powers. Ravana's men followed up with hypodermic needles that knocked them out. By the time they woke up they were in the cell in Ravana's building.

So began days of torture and pain. Installed into the walls of the cell were emitters that created a dampening effect on their powers. Doctor Ravana called it a zeno ray. The chamber also had torture pads built into the floor so Ravana only had to flip a switch and they would be hit by the intense waves of agony.

The thought of it makes me sick.

'I wanted to kill Ravana,' Chad says. 'He deserved to die for what he did to us.'

I find it hard to argue the point with him. Ravana is the sort of monster you want to see put into jail and the key thrown away.

But we're not killers.

'A lot of people probably deserve to die,' I tell Chad. 'But that's not our call.'

He looks like he wants to argue. 'Anyway, it looks like Ravana is permanently out of the equation now.'

I think back to the burning figure on the building. 'Probably. Although, he has a habit of turning up like a bad penny.'

Brodie's head pokes in through the door. 'Are you boys still comparing your muscles or are you ready for breakfast?'

I realize I'm famished. 'Show me the food.'

Ten minutes later we're sitting around eating pancakes and bacon. It's the perfect combination of fat and sugar. This type of food won't sustain you long term, but it's perfect when recovering from bullet wounds and sadistic maniacs.

Halfway through breakfast there's another knock at the door.

'Did you order more room service?' I ask Dan.

He shakes his head.

Worried, I insist on answering. I'm not in the best shape, but at least I can protect myself with a barrier if someone starts shooting. When I open the door I find a man standing there. He doesn't look like he wants to shoot me. That's a start.

He's tall and thin and wearing a dark suit. He has black hair, cut short at the sides and a thin mustache.

'May I come in?' he asks.

Before I can answer, he steps past me and walks into the apartment. He casts an eye across everyone in the room.

'My name is Mr Jones,' he says. 'I'm with The Agency.'

Chapter Nineteen

'May I sit down?' he asks.

Seeing as how he didn't mind walking in on us without waiting for an invitation, it seems nice that he asks for a chair. I point him to one. Everyone stares at him in amazement. If I could take a photo it would show Brodie with her mouth wide open, Dan frozen in position with a forkful of food, Ebony with eyes like saucers and Chad—well, nothing much impresses him. He simply raises his eyebrows for a few seconds. Then he glares at Jones like he's an unwelcome guest.

Which he may well be.

'This is a nice pad you've got here,' Jones says. 'Who picked the apartment?'

Dan holds up the fork. A piece of pancake slides off it onto the floor.

'You've got class, kid,' he says.

'Thanks.'

'Enough of this bull!' Chad snaps. 'Who are you and what are you doing here?'

Chad looks so threatening even I feel a little concerned. I keep remembering that burst of fire that engulfed Ravana back at the building. Jones, however, regards him with little more than a curious expression. He looks him up and down before leaning forward and clasping his hands together.

'Chad,' he says. 'It's been a long time.'

How he knows Chad's name is beyond me.

'You can cut the riddles,' Brodie says. 'We want some answers.'

Jones nods. 'You deserve that. Especially after everything you've been through. Although there are some gaps in your knowledge I can fill and other items that will forever remain a mystery.'

'Our names,' I interrupt. 'What are our names? Our real names.'

The man in the suit gives a sad smile. 'Unfortunately, I don't have that information. Very few people do.'

'And what happened to our memories?' Dan asks. 'Why can't we remember who we are?'

Jones holds up a hand. 'Let me explain,' he

said. 'First of all, you are part of a venture known as The Alpha Project. The name of the project has a number of meanings. Alpha is the first of its kind. Alpha is also short for alphabet. Your names—your chosen names—are derived from the alphabet.'

I'm already confused. 'What does that mean exactly?'

'Axel, Brodie, Chad, Dan and Ebony.' He paused. 'Do you notice anything? Your names are—'

'The first five letters of the alphabet,' I finish. 'A, B, C, D and E.'

We sit in silence for a moment.

'The Alpha Project is one of the many scientific endeavors carried out by The Agency,' Jones explained. 'The scientists involved assembled a group of orphaned children to create a new form of modified human.'

Dan starts. 'And The Agency is…'

Jones sighs. 'There are a few pieces of information I'm about to disseminate that are going to change your whole view of the world.'

We all look at each other.

'Sure,' I say.

He studies our faces one by one. 'Okay. Here it is.' For a moment he looks like he would rather not continue. Finally, he says, 'Aliens are here on Earth. They've been on Earth for thousands of years. They are a race known as the Bakari. The Agency was started by the Bakari to monitor and guide our activities.'

No-one says anything.

Mr Jones continues. 'One day we're joining the galactic club. We'll be a fully fledged member of everything that's out there. Until then they're helping us develop technologies to get ready for that day.'

Still, no-one says anything.

'Mostly they leave us to our own affairs. They don't want to interfere with our internal politics, but nor do they want us to destroy ourselves,' Mr Jones continues. 'That would be a waste. They want us to help ourselves, which is why they started the Alpha Project. All of you were modified to make the world a better place. To help save us from ourselves.'

Mr Jones stops and studies our faces. 'That's

about it. Does anyone have any questions?'

'I do,' Chad says. 'Is there any pizza left over from last night?'

I ignore him. 'How come no-one's ever heard of The Agency? How could something like this be kept secret?'

'They have their methods,' Mr Jones says. 'As I say, they like to observe. They don't want to interfere.'

'But they were happy to experiment on us,' Chad says.

'For the greater good,' Mr Jones replies.

'And we're orphans,' Brodie says.

He nods. 'You were all chosen because your parents had died or abandoned you. Some of you were in orphanages. Some were in juvenile prisons. We needed children we could use for the Alpha trials.'

'You mean guinea pigs,' Chad interrupts.

Jones levels a gaze at him. 'You all signed paperwork consenting to the procedure. We needed teenagers because your bodies are still in a state of growth. Adult tissue, as the scientists involved in the project found, would not work. The adult test subjects did not survive.'

Brodie laughs hollowly. 'We signed paperwork? But we have no memory of consenting to these procedures. How convenient.'

'I assure you we explained the process in full,' he says. 'I'm told you were all most enthusiastic. And why not? You were promised powers far beyond those that any human has ever possessed.'

'You made us…superheroes,' Dan says as if he's trying to assimilate this information one piece at a time. 'And there are aliens on Earth. Do they have two heads? Are they grays like in the movies?'

'They look just like you and me,' Mr Jones says. 'Identical.'

'And you operated on us…' Ebony says.

Jones nods. 'The scientists in charge of the Alpha Project made you superheroes. The combination of drugs and implants were designed to react naturally with your own latent genetic abilities.' He looks at Brodie. 'You were naturally fast and lithe, so you became even more so. Axel rated highly in terms of psychic abilities. So did Dan and Chad.'

'But I can make fire and ice,' Chad protests. 'And Ebony can transmute substances. What sort of latent genetic abilities are those?'

'Those are abilities that have been long lost and forgotten,' Jones says. 'Some of our ancestors had these abilities millennia ago, but these genes were disseminated throughout the gene pool. The Alpha Project reactivated those genetic markers.'

I shake my head. This is all too much. It's crazy. It means I have no family. It means my name was stolen from me. It means I once agreed to be pumped full of drugs because I wanted to be some kind of…superhero. It means every human being has latent incredible powers.

It means there are aliens on Earth.

Aliens.

'So how did I end up in a seedy hotel room?' I ask. 'What the hell went wrong?'

'Our security went wrong,' Jones says grimly. 'An organization known as Typhoid infiltrated The

Agency with the intention of killing all of you. You would have been killed, but a group of scientists, led by a man named Doctor Richards, secreted your group out of the facility to save your lives.

'They were uncertain as to whom they could trust, so they planned to reassemble once the crisis had passed at The Agency. Unfortunately, Typhoid was ahead of us and ambushed the scientists at a meeting. Most of them were killed.'

'Was that Doctor Richards in the hotel room?' I ask. 'He was injured and died shortly after I awoke.'

Jones nods. 'We believe he survived the attack and returned to the hotel.'

'Still,' Chad frowns. 'We were abandoned in warehouses and hotels all over the city with no memories and no-one to turn to. That's not much of a save.'

'For the scientists involved it was that or certain death,' Jones points out. 'I'm sure you prefer their poor solution to no solution at all.'

I think back to the man on the floor of the hotel room. It all seems so long ago. Like it all happened to a different person. I almost ask Jones about the meaning of the book and the strange device we found inside it, except I remember Richards' advice.

Trust no-one.

Some…at The Agency…will help you.

Some at The Agency will help us. That might not necessarily include Mr Jones. Or maybe it does. Regardless, the best way to handle this is quietly. Dan has displayed some psychic abilities. Maybe they will stretch to determining who is on our side and who is a traitor.

'So what happens now?' I ask.

'That's a good question,' Jones says. 'It has taken us some time to track you down. Now you have to come back to the facility to complete your training.'

'Really?' Chad gives him a mocking grin. 'I like things exactly as they are.'

Jones does a pretty good job of containing his cool. If Chad has a superpower, it's pissing people off. I agree with Chad and I still want to punch him in the face.

'You have all signed waivers,' Jones says. 'You belong to us whether you like it or not.'

'I belong to me,' Chad says.

'We don't want to force you back,' Jones says. 'Twelve, in particular, wants you back to assist with a mission.'

'Twelve—what?' Brodie asks.

'He's known as Twelve,' Mr Jones says. 'He's—'

'Don't tell me,' Chad says. 'He's an alien.'

'That's correct.'

'I knew they'd come into it sooner or later. I'd like to see you try to force us back.'

'I hope it will not come to that.' The agent looks like he's about to try a different approach when there's a knock at the door. Dan jumps up to answer it.

'That must be the ice cream I ordered,' he says.

'You ordered ice cream for breakfast?' I ask incredulously.

'Absolutely,' he says. 'You know, eat, drink and eat ice-cream for tomorrow we die?'

Brodie shakes her head in disbelief. 'I don't think it quite goes like that.'

Dan opens the door. One of the serving carts is sitting outside. The attendant has already gone. As Dan wheels it in I'm thinking how strange it is that room service has abandoned the cartload of food.

Daniel reaches for the serving cover.

No!

The cart explodes.

Chapter Twenty

I have to say it is luck more than ability that enables me to get my shield up in time. It's simply an instinct that makes me enable it just as Dan lifts the serving cover. Even then it's not at full strength. In the split second that I see the burst of light emanate from the cart, I strengthen the shield.

Still, we are all thrown in all directions. At some point I am knocked out by the blast. Probably I'm only out for a few seconds. It seems longer. I'm still struggling to get to my feet when I realize Jones is helping me up.

He says something, but I'm still too woozy to make it out.

'Whassat?' I ask.

'You saved us, kid,' he says. 'All of us.'

'Don't call me kid,' I tell him. 'My name's Axel.'

Although it could be Frank or Joe or Bill or anything, really.

Who knows?

'Axel.' He clasps my shoulder. 'Thank you.'

I begin to look around and only now appreciate the level of devastation. Whatever was packed into that cart was designed to blow us to kingdom come. Windows. Walls. Carpets. Everything is black and smoking or blasted into nothing.

Chad is helping his sister up. Brodie is walking around looking dazed. Dan—poor Dan—is picking himself up off the floor. He is still holding onto the handle of the food cover. Attached to the handle is about six inches of the cover. Where the food cart was is just a hole in the ground.

If I hadn't become suspicious at the last moment, we'd be dead. I shake my head. I don't want to even think about it.

'Are you responsible for this?' Chad turns on Mr Jones. 'Did you try to kill us?'

Jones shakes his head in disbelief. 'You just don't get it, do you kid? I'm here to help you. Save you.' For the first time Jones actually looks angry. 'This was Ravana and his group. They're going to keep on trying to kill you until they succeed. There's only one way for you to survive this.'

'And how's that?' Brodie asks.

'You need to come with me,' Jones says. 'You need to get trained so you can fight Typhoid.'

'And if we don't?' Ebony asks.

As far as I can remember, this is the first time she has spoken. She looks shaken from the explosion, but not weakened. I suspect there is quite a strong character residing beneath this quiet exterior.

'Then I can't guarantee your safety.' Jones spreads his hands. 'Look around you. Typhoid almost got you this time. It's only because of Axel's powers that we survived. And if you don't care about your own safety, what about the safety of everyone else?'

I notice the sound of sirens drawing closer. I realize there must be debris from the explosion spread out over a radius of hundreds of feet. Maybe there are already injured or dying people on the street below.

Jones is right about one thing. Being located in the middle of the city is dangerous for everyone concerned.

Strangely, it is Chad who speaks for all of us.

'Okay,' he says. 'We'll do it your way, but don't think we intend to be your puppets.'

I give a laugh. 'It's hard to imagine you as a puppet, Chad.'

'Very funny.'

'We need to get out of here,' Jones says. The sirens are drawing closer. The police will be here in seconds asking questions that nobody wants to answer. 'There is a van down stairs waiting for us. We'd best take the stairs.'

It turns out the stairs are not only a good option, but they're the *only* option. The elevators are not operating since the blast. We encounter people evacuating the building on the way down. It's eerily reminiscent of our attack on Ravana's building, but this time we're the ones getting evacuated.

A few minutes later we're on the street. There's a large delivery truck parked at the side of the road. A door is built into the side of it which seems a little strange; most of these vehicles only seem to open from the rear. A truck driver jumps out of the cab, rounds the vehicle and unlocks the door.

Peering at the outside of the vehicle, I turn to Brodie. 'Looks like we're traveling in style.'

'No doubt.'

Strangely, despite my sarcasm, the interior is exactly that. You've probably seen those amazing campervans that people have which are like little homes on wheels; they have lounge chairs, marble topped kitchen benches, oak wardrobes, television and DVD players. Everything is a little shrunk as if they expect the occupants to be escapees from The Wizard of Oz, but they're certainly built for comfort.

This place is like one of those vans. Except it has no windows.

That's slightly disconcerting, but we file in and attempt to make ourselves comfortable. It seems that Dan has an insatiable appetite. No sooner are we seated in respective corners of the van than he is searching through the fridge for something to eat.

'Really?' I say to him. 'You're hungry?'

He looks at me completely straight faced. 'Someone blew up my ice cream.'

Can't argue with that.

Shaking my head in disbelief, I look for somewhere to sit. There's a place next to Ebony. I give her a slight smile and she nods slightly. I'm not sure what to say to her. We've been through a lot together in a short time, but I barely know her. I consider trying to act cool, but end up with dorky instead.

I hold out a hand. 'Hi. I'm Axel.'

She looks at me as if I'm slightly mad. Maybe I am.

'Uh, yeah, I'm Ebony.' She seems stuck for words. 'We've already met. Did you hit your head or something?'

'No, I'm just kidding around.'

Well, that exchange has worked just fine. Now she thinks I'm a crazy person. Yep, I'm a real ladies man. No doubt about that. I'm beginning to suspect I had as little success in my pre-hero life as I do now.

'How long do you think this is going to take?' she asks.

'I don't know.' I'm glad she's decided to ignore my gawkiness. 'Mr Jones said something about it taking several hours to get to the base.'

Ebony lets out a long sigh. She seems so fragile. It's hard to believe she is part of this superhero squad. Typhoid seems pretty intent on killing us all. Maybe she would be happier retiring to a little town in the country and becoming a librarian. She seems that type.

'Maybe you won't have to fight,' I say suddenly. 'I mean, if you don't want to.'

She looks at me, confused. 'I don't know what you mean.'

'I'm just saying, well, you didn't choose to be here and you might want out.'

Ebony frowns. 'Where would I go?'

That's a good question. It's a big, bad wide world out there and particularly tough for someone with no family, no friends and no visible means of support.

Hell, where would any of us go?

Suddenly I notice a mark on the back of Ebony's hand. It's a burn.

'What happened to your hand?' I examine it.

'Was that from the blast?'

She nods. 'It's okay.'

'You should have gotten it checked out.'

At that moment, Brodie comes over and sees me holding Ebony's hand.

'Everything okay?' she asks.

'Sure. I just noticed Ebony's got a burn on her hand.'

'Really?'

I don't like the accusatory tone in Brodie's voice.

Yes. Really, I think. *Why else would I be holding hands with her?*

'You should get that checked out,' Brodie says.

'I will,' Ebony says. 'I'll get them to look at it when we reach the facility.'

Brodie shoots a look at me. I suspect she wants to hit me or something, but I have no idea why.

The following hours pass slowly. There are a couple of books in the van, but none of them are page turners. The television is still showing all the same old junk. It turns out the truck only has sleeping areas for two, so the rest of us simply crash out in the chairs where we're seated.

Chad comes over to where I'm slouched.

'Got any ideas about where we're headed?' he asks.

I shrug. 'I'm not sure. Probably some sort of military base.'

'I think we're going to South Carolina.'

'What's in South Carolina?' I ask.

'There's a major military base at Charleston,' he says. 'It would be easy for an organization like The Agency to work in conjunction with the American government.'

'You think The Agency is working with the government?'

'Sure it is. Haven't you seen *Men in Black*? Haven't you seen all the conspiracy stuff on the net about secret societies and the New World Order?'

'You think the government is in on this whole thing?'

He shrugs. 'Who knows? But I'm not trusting

any of them.'

No argument there. 'So you think we're going to South Carolina? It's hard to tell what's going on from inside this truck. We could be sitting in a car park with the engine running for all we know.'

'You watch,' he says. 'It's Charleston.'

I nod. After a while I close my eyes and an indeterminable time passes. Finally I'm jolted into wakefulness. At first I wonder what's brought me back to life from the Land of Nod, but then I know. The truck has come to a halt. No sooner do we look blearily at each other than the back of the truck starts to disengage. It slowly eases down into a ramp and we find ourselves parked in an underground facility illuminated by stark artificial lights.

Mr Jones is waiting at the foot of the ramp.

'Welcome to The Agency,' he says.

Chapter Twenty-One

I glance at my watch. Chad could be right about the Charleston suggestion. We've been traveling about half a day in total. The little I can see of the facility looks like a military installation. It feels like some sort of huge nuclear bunker in case of war. I mention it to Jones as we walk away from the truck.

'You're not too far wrong,' he says. 'The Agency has a number of similar bunkers spread across the planet. They're used for a variety of purposes. Mostly experimentation. Research. And watching. Always watching.'

'So how does the government fit into all this?' I decide to ask him straight out. 'How involved are they?'

'The Agency is independent of all government bodies,' he says. 'They're ignorant—mostly—of our existence.'

'Mostly?'

'The Agency has been around for centuries,' he says. 'It's hard to keep a secret for that long.'

I begin to wonder about all those people talking about alien abductions over the years. And experimentation. Maybe they're not so crazy after all.

We leave the tunnel where the truck is parked and enter an enormous cave that's larger than a football stadium. There are high tech devices all over the place. Odd looking aircraft. Computer systems. There are pieces of machinery that look like weapons, but I have no idea what they would do.

There are also people everywhere. It's like Grand Central Station. They're going in all different directions. Most of them appear to be scientists; they're dressed in white lab coats. Others look like administrative workers. There are no soldiers to be seen. This is obviously not a military installation.

'This area is known as The Cavern,' Jones explains. 'Among other things, the ceiling opens up for VTOL—Vertical Take Off and Landing—aircraft.'

'And the American government just lets you work down here,' Chad says, shooting me a look.

Mr Jones sighs. 'I'll just say that we have

people in the government who make certain that this piece of real estate remains undeveloped.'

Chad asks Mr Jones about a strange platform erected vertically on top of one of the trucks.

'That's an interesting one to ask about,' Jones says. 'It's a teleportation device that transports you out of this dimension.'

'Transports you?' Ebony asks. 'Transports you *where*?'

Jones shakes his head. 'They're not really sure. That's why it's still experimental.'

We enter a long tunnel where a jeep is awaiting us. We climb in and it takes us up the passage until it stops outside a concrete structure built into the rock. It reminds me of those ancient Indian ruins like Montezuma's Castle. We pile out and follow Jones into an office. An administrative guy is seated at the reception desk.

'Hey Wally,' Jones says. 'We're here to see Twelve.'

Wally the receptionist has another name. His name badge says he is Mr Evans. He looks none too happy about being referred to as Wally, but he ignores the remark and looks past him at us. 'So our little birds have returned to the coop.'

Jones smiles without the slightest trace of humor. 'Just tell Twelve we're here.'

The receptionist doesn't even look at him. Wally simply picks up a phone and speaks quietly into it. A moment later he puts it down and turns back to us.

'You can go in now,' Wally says. 'Twelve has been waiting for you.'

The way he says this last sentence makes it sound like we've kept Twelve waiting. This could be interesting.

We follow Mr Jones into the office. The Agency Chief has the courtesy to stand as we file in and take seats. I notice Ebony looks a little scared. Brodie looks concerned. Dan is in awe of the whole experience. Chad looks like—

Well, he's Chad. He always looks like he's searching for a fight.

'Good afternoon,' the man says. 'I'm Twelve.'

He doesn't look like an alien. Actually there are victims of Hollywood plastic surgeons who look more like aliens than this guy. Twelve appears to be about sixty years old. He's clean shaven with a crew cut. Graying hair. Doesn't smile. You wouldn't look twice at him if you passed him on the street.

We all sort of grunt something in reply.

'We have actually met before,' he continues. 'But I understand your memories have been wiped as part of the genetic engineering of your cells. First of all I want to thank you for agreeing to help us. The last few days must have been very confusing for you.'

'Confusing is an understatement,' Dan says.

The alien gives something approaching a smile. 'I'm sorry about the difficulties you've endured. The Agency is a big organization with many branches. It was sadly inevitable that a rogue organization would infiltrate us sooner or later.' He pauses. 'I believe Mr Jones has already told you about Typhoid.'

'A little,' Brodie says.

He nods. 'Typhoid is a mercenary

organization willing to sell its skills to the highest bidder. They have been implicated in a number of operations over the years including the assassination of the Swedish Prime Minister, a wave of bombings in Iraq and the destruction of a passenger jet over the Atlantic last year, killing three hundred and nine passengers and crew.

'It goes without saying they are both a ruthless and dangerous organization. We need your assistance to stop them in their latest mission.'

We all look at each other. Chad finally asks, 'And what is that mission, Mr, uh, Twelve?'

'Just Twelve will suffice,' he says without smiling. 'As you are probably aware, the distribution of plutonium is rigidly controlled by world governments because of its possible use in nuclear weapons.

'Despite their best efforts, we believe that Typhoid recently acquired a quantity of weapons grade plutonium from a disgruntled employee within the former USSR.

'That alone would be a cause of immense

concern,' Twelve says. 'But to make matters even worse, about a year ago an experimental missile was stolen from a high security facility in Atlanta. The missile is known as Pegasus.'

'As in the winged horse?' Brodie asks.

Twelve nods. 'Pegasus is the first missile ever to be installed with a full range of stealth capabilities. It can avoid radar detection as well as dramatically reduce audio, visual, radio and infrared visibility.

'We believe Typhoid have processed the plutonium, constructed a nuclear warhead and are preparing to install it into Pegasus. In short, the missile will become the perfect weapon. With a reach of half the globe as well as being able to reach speeds of up to Mach 3, it will be able to strike at ease.'

'Which means..?' Chad's voice trailed off.

'I'm talking a fully equipped nuclear weapon,' Twelve confirms. 'It has come to our attention that a terrorist organization recently paid some one billion dollars to Typhoid to target Pegasus at an American city.

'We need your assistance to stop that

happening.'

Brodie frowns. 'I'm sure we're more than happy to help out, but I'm not sure we can.' She quickly looks to the rest of us. Only Chad looks like he wants to disagree. 'Surely with your advanced alien technology you could—'

Twelve interrupts. 'We are watchers. Observers. Our role is to track the progress of humanity without interfering. Having said that, we have no desire to see millions of people die. Humans have to look after their own problems. You have, after all, created most of them.'

He pauses. 'This is one reason why we developed the Alpha Project. To give humanity an edge against destructive devices such as this.'

'So where's this missile?' Chad asks.

'It is being held on a small island called Cayo Placetas.'

'So why not just tell the American military?' Chad asks. 'Or NATO or someone.'

'That's not the role of The Agency,' Twelve says. 'We don't work with government agencies.

Besides, Cayo Placetas is part of Cuba. The United States will not attack a foreign country without provocation—especially Cuba—and officially we have no evidence that Typhoid is operating from the island.

'But, you see, we have something Typhoid doesn't have.'

'And what's that?' I ask.

'We have you. Typhoid agents are highly trained operatives, but they don't have extraordinary powers. They don't have 'super' powers. This is why Typhoid attacked The Agency. Through a leak in our security they found out about you and decided to remove you from the equation. We want to land you on Cayo Placetas because we believe you can destroy the guidance system before Pegasus is ready to fire.

'And what if we get caught?' Brodie asks. 'What's to stop us from blabbing about The Agency, aliens and everything else you've told us?'

'You have a shut off switch,' Mr Jones says.

'A what?' I ask.

'Sorry,' Jones apologizes. 'Let me rephrase

that. You have a poisonous capsule inserted under your skin that can be activated by remote control. It will kill you instantly.'

Well, that's a downer, I think. And things were going so well up till now.

'Your bodies will degrade at a rate far more quickly than normal,' Jones continues. 'It will be impossible for experiments to be carried out on your dead tissue by Typhoid or any foreign government, for that matter.'

'You really know how to sell a car,' Chad says.

'I won't gloss over how serious this is,' Twelve continues. 'This is a highly dangerous mission. You may even die.' He pauses. 'But you will save millions of lives.'

'So how would we destroy Pegasus?' Brodie asks. 'Providing we agree to this deadly mission.'

Mr Jones takes over. 'Fortunately Pegasus has one glaring weakness. Its guidance system is operated solely from a computer on the island. It will be impossible to fire the weapon if the computer system is destroyed.'

'So we only need to destroy the computer,' Dan says. 'Providing we go.'

Twelve leans back in his chair. 'I am prepared to offer you a deal I would certainly not offer anyone else.'

'And that's that?' Brodie asks.

'Technically, you belong to The Agency.'

'I don't belong to anyone,' Chad cuts in angrily. 'I certainly—'

Twelve holds up his hand. 'I might remind you that no-one even knows of your existence. As far as the outside world is concerned, you have ceased to exist. If you were to refuse to carry out this assignment we could kill you immediately.'

'And if we should carry out this mission?' I ask.

'You will be free to resume your lives,' he says. 'The poisonous capsules in your bodies will be deactivated. You can start afresh. Your lives will be your own to live without having to worry about The Agency or Typhoid ever again.'

Chad sits forward. 'That sounds like a carrot and stick proposal. A carrot to move us forward while a stick threatens us from behind.'

'You may see it that way if you wish.' Twelve lets the words hang in the air. 'We've watched the human race for centuries as you've fought your wars and committed genocide against each other. Our role is to observe. If you don't agree to this assignment, then millions of people will die. We would prefer not to observe that particular atrocity.'

No-one says anything for a while.

Finally I say, 'Providing we decide to carry out this assignment, how long do you have to get ready?'

'About three weeks,' Jones says. 'Certainly no longer.'

Three weeks. It doesn't seem like a long time. Still, we do have super powers and we were able to help Chad and Ebony escape with no training at all.

Twelve picks up his phone. 'Has Doctor Sokolov arrived yet?' He nods. 'Good. Show her in.'

An attractive woman, slim bodied with black

hair and round rimmed glasses enters the room carrying a clipboard and files. I notice she has dark rings around her eyes. Either she parties too much or gets too little sleep.

'Twelve,' she nods.

'Project Alpha,' Twelve says. 'Doctor Anna Sokolov will be in charge of your progress here at The Agency.'

'It's good to see you again,' the doctor says.

'We've met before?' Brodie asks skeptically.

'I initiated you into The Agency when you first arrived,' she says. 'Now you must begin the next step of your training.'

Judging by her name, I assume she is Russian, but her accent is very faint. I look closely at her face. She is a beautiful woman. Possibly about twenty-five years old. She's so attractive I find it hard to believe I could forget someone like that. I glance over at Chad. I stifle a grin. If he were a wolf, he would be salivating.

'I will take you to your quarters,' she says. 'I advise you to get a good night's sleep. Your training starts tomorrow.'

'It won't be anything we can't handle,' Chad laughs.

'We shall see,' the doctor replies. 'We shall see.'

Chapter Twenty-Two

When the alarm goes off, it's like a bomb exploding in my head. To make matters worse, it's accompanied by the flickering of fluorescent lights in the ceiling. One second I'm sound asleep in complete darkness. The next I feel like an insect being studied under a magnifying glass.

I blearily examine the alarm clock.

5.30am

Oh, God.

The previous night I found myself housed in a dorm room with Chad and Dan while Brodie and Ebony were given a room across the hall. Compared to our previous penthouse accommodation, this place is more like Guantanamo Bay. Everything is concrete. There are no windows because we are still a hundred feet underground. The beds are reinforced steel bunks. There are no pictures on the walls. Even the television looks like it was built during the Cold War.

I had half expected to find pajamas made to look like orange jumpsuits, but they turn out to be military green tops and shorts.

As I sit up in the bed I find myself wondering one thing.

What have I gotten myself into?

I suddenly hear the shower running. I look blearily over at Dan and Chad who look even worse than me. A computerized voice emanates from a loudspeaker built into the ceiling.

'The shower provides hot water for three minutes,' it informs us. 'After that it converts to cold water only.'

You've got to be kidding.

The three of us charge madly for the shower, but Chad gets there first. I don't think he's ever showered with two guys watching him.

'What're you looking at?' he asks, rubbing soap all over him.

'Two minutes,' the computer intones.

'Out!' I yell. 'Get out!'

We virtually drag him out by the hair. I jump in next, promising I'll give Dan his full minute. Before I'm even half washed, though, the computer announces the shower has one minute of hot water remaining.

Dan glowers at me.

'Aw, hell,' I say, climbing out.

I dry myself and drag on clothes. As soon as Dan finishes his shower, cold and shivering, the computer tells us breakfast will be served in five minutes in Kitchen Twelve. I remember the location from Anna's tour the previous evening. It's about two hundred feet down the hallway.

The computer continues.

'Breakfast will begin at five forty-five am and will conclude at five fifty-five am.'

I have to think really hard about what the computer has said because my head is still in bed while the rest of me is only pretending to be awake.

'That's ten minutes,' I say aloud. 'Ten minutes for breakfast.'

We charge out of there and bump into the girls in the hallway. They look like they've just escaped a flooded building. Neither has combed her hair. Ebony's is still dripping wet.

'We had three minutes for both of us to shower!' Brodie yells.

'Three minutes?' I yell. There's some sort of inequality here. 'Between the two of you? That means you had an entire minute and a half per person. We only had a minute!'

'Bad luck!' Brodie snaps.

No-one speaks during breakfast. There are three attendants bringing food out to us like clockwork. And there's plenty of it. Sausages, eggs, bacon, toast, oat meal. The list goes on. We find we're stuffing it in as fast as we can. Who knows where our next meal is coming from?

This is insane. I remember the nice abandoned warehouse I shared with Brodie that first night. The cold, damp building with rats eyeing us hungrily from the corners. It was like heaven compared to this. I catch her eye and I'm sure she's thinking the same thing.

'Remember the good old days?' I ask her.

She shakes her head and a lock of hair bounces in front of her eyes.

'Just eat,' she replies.

Our drill instructor turns out to be a large black man by the name of Mr Henderson. It seems that no-one here has first names. I don't think his mother ever taught him how to smile. If she did, his knowledge of it is hidden beneath a permanent scowl. He takes us outside via an elevator housed in a concrete bunker that opens up to reveal a large field. Rolling hills surround it on all sides. It's all very picturesque.

'Where are we?' I ask.

He ignores me completely. 'I will be your physical exercise instructor. I have three weeks to beat you recruits into shape. That's not much time. That means you'll have to follow my every command if you want to be ready in time.'

'What if I don't plan to be ready?' Chad asks, smiling.

What is it with this guy?

'You don't want to find out,' Henderson says.

I believe him.

We start with a three mile run following a

track through the woods. It was a beautiful morning in a beautiful part of the country. How horrible to ruin it with exercise. By the time I'm halfway around I'm regretting eating so much at breakfast. As we get back to the bunker I'm pretty sure I'm about to see breakfast again at close hand. After that we move onto pushups and sit ups. Around about that time breakfast makes a return visit for me, Dan and Ebony. Chad takes a little longer to crack. It's on the second run that he empties his stomach. Brodie makes it through everything unscathed.

I realize around about this time that Brodie has a natural advantage in all these exercises. Whereas the rest of us have powers that involve the manipulation of external elements, her power is purely physiological.

Damn.

We stop for lunch and this time the meal break is a far more leisurely affair. No-one speaks. Dan doesn't eat anything. I think it's the first time I've seen him reject food. Even Chad barely touches a thing.

We all get separated after lunch. My personal trainer is a man named Mr Brown. He's like Henderson, but a smaller and stockier version, if such a thing is possible. He's dressed in a tracksuit like a personal trainer, but he looks like a military guy. He's well versed in all my powers. He begins by getting me to produce shields of various sizes. Small. Large. Then he gets me to morph them into different shapes.

I move onto flying. He doesn't get me to fly any great distances. Quite the opposite. He hones me in covering short areas, but doing it with skill. Sometimes I'm just hovering bare inches above the ground. At other times I fly upside down and do complete somersaults. After I've done this for an hour I remind him I'm capable of flying quite high.

'I'm well aware of that, recruit,' he informs me.

It seems he has either forgotten my name or doesn't intend to use it.

'You need to polish your basic skills before you move onto advanced moves.' He gives me the closest thing to a smile I'm likely to see. 'Baby steps, recruit. Baby steps.'

The day's activities end with me creating air weapons. First I make balls and throw them. Then I move onto darts. In the last hour he shows me pictures of a Japanese throwing star called a shuriken and gets me to create and throw them at targets.

'So when do I get a break?' I ask him.

'You can relax when I say you can,' he replies, smiling.

That's not a pleasant smile.

By the time I head back to the facility for dinner I'm just about falling over my own feet. I'm physically and mentally exhausted. I stumble into the dining room and the catering attendants start piling food in front of me. The others look the same. Poor Dan looks like he's about to pass out. Ebony looks ill. Even Chad looks tired.

Brodie…well, what should I say?

'How was your day?' she asks me brightly, throwing back food like she hasn't eaten for three days.

'Great…great…'

'Feel like a run after dinner?' she suggests. 'Nothing like a quick ten mile jog to polish off a perfect day.'

She's so evil.

After dinner we have free time. For every one of us, even Brodie despite her suggestion of another run, free time equals sleep time. We get shown the location of an entertainment room with a wide-screened television. There's even a games room with the latest computer hardware, but no-one shows the slightest interest.

Later, I remember climbing into my pajamas. I remember falling into bed. I remember closing my eyes.

I don't remember anything after that.

Chapter Twenty-Three

I'd like to say the following week gets easier.

It doesn't.

There are some improvements. The showers are still three minutes long and we get better at jumping in, scrubbing ourselves raw and climbing out to make room for the next person. We learn to eat less for breakfast, more for lunch and finish with a large dinner. As far as everything else goes, it's still a nightmare.

The physical regime is incrementally increased each day. The run is increased by only a few hundred feet, but you know about it. Then there are more sit ups and pushups. Mr Henderson seems to only know three words—faster, harder and faster.

Okay, that's two words, but you get the idea.

Even the afternoons spent honing our skills become a chore. Every day it gets harder. Every day it's more demanding. As soon as I master one skill, Mr Brown gets me to move onto something else.

After a few days he gets me to start combining

my skills. I have to stay in flight, while creating a barrier as I throw invisible balls at a moving target. The whole thing gives me a headache.

Finally he starts me off on speed and distance trials. He gets me to go straight up as fast and as high as possible. It turns out to be the one single highpoint of the training. He fits me out with a small device that registers height and speed. I have to wear a special suit to keep me warm. In addition, he teaches me a method to continue breathing at high altitudes.

The first time I do it I err on the side of caution. By the time I return to Earth, Brown is waiting for me with a frown on his face.

'You call that fast?' Mr Brown asks. 'I want that sound barrier broken, recruit.'

'Yes, sir!'

I take flight again and give it all I've got. This time I go so high the sky starts to turn an indigo shade of blue. This time when I return to base Mr Brown is looking at a small hand held data pad.

'You broke Mach One today,' he informs me. 'Tomorrow we'll try for Mach Two.'

On the eighth day I stumble into the dinner hall and the catering assistants start the evening ritual of piling food before us. I have to give The Agency credit for one thing. They know how to build a healthy body. I have muscles I never knew existed. I have also learnt the gentle art of running without vomiting.

Hey, that's a good thing.

During dinner, Chad keeps on trying to catch my eye. When the catering assistants return to the kitchen he leans across the table to me.

'We need to talk,' he says.

'About what?'

He eyes the kitchen staff suspiciously. 'Later.'

As we leave the hall I make certain I lag behind with Chad. We find a quiet recess leading off one of the corridors. I wonder why he drags me in here until I realize there are no cameras covering this part of the facility. Just about every square inch of The Agency is monitored.

Even then, he looks around carefully for listening devices.

'Okay,' he says finally. 'I think we can talk.'

'What's this all about?'

He leans close. 'It's about this place. It's Stalag 13! It's a nightmare. I'm getting out of here.'

'You must be joking.' I shake my head. 'This place is more secure than Fort Knox. And what about Ebony?'

'I'm not leaving forever,' he says. 'I just need to get out of here for twenty-four hours.'

'You're mad,' I tell him.

'I want you to come too.' His mouth turns into a smile. 'I can't party on my own. There must be a town around here. We can get some booze. Listen to some music.'

'No way!'

'What are you? A saint?'

'I just don't want to get into trouble!'

'Get a life!' He pokes me in the chest. 'This place is run by aliens and mad scientists. They're not in control of our lives. We are.'

'And what about the poison capsules they inserted into our bodies?'

'They're not going to kill us for just blowing off some steam.'

I turn my back on him. 'I'm going to bed.'

Neither of us speak as we make our way back to the dorm rooms. Dan looks at us curiously.

'What were you guys talking about?' he asks.

'Nothing!' Chad snaps.

We get ready for bed and turn the lights out. At first I lie awake and stare at the ceiling. My eyes stray to the clock. I don't want Chad to screw everything up for all of us. Despite the hardships of the last week, I know my powers are stronger and more refined by being here than if I had been doing this alone for a year.

My eyes grow sleepy as I stare at the clock.

10:00pm.

Darkness.

My eyes slowly creak open and I realize it's still night. This is the first time I've woken without the lights snapping to attention since we started here. At first I'm confused. I have no idea what's going on. Why aren't I asleep?

Then I hear the muffled sound of clothing in the dark.

Chad.

I climb out of bed and fumble around. I turn on a light. Chad already has his clothing on and is pulling on shoes.

'Hey amigo,' he says cheerily. 'Coming out to play?'

'You're insane,' I hiss. 'You're just going to get all of us in trouble.'

'Are you coming with me or not?'

I sit on the edge of the bed and stare down at the floor. This is a stupid idea. We need to be getting ready to take on Typhoid. Going out to party is insane. However, there's a nagging sensation in the back of my brain. I haven't really taken too kindly to being a prisoner here. The image of Mr Brown telling me we can have a break when he decides…

Look, I tell myself. How bad can it be? Even if we get caught we'll just make light of it and tell them we'll be good boys from now on. Besides, they need us more than we need them.

'Okay,' I nod. 'I'm coming with you.'

'Good man!' Chad just about punches the air.

Dan stirs at that moment and sits up. 'I bag's first shower.'

'Go back to sleep,' I say.

He does. I drag my gear on and we make our way to the door. Chad peeks out. A few seconds later I hear a low crackling sound.

'Okay,' he enters the passageway. 'Follow me.'

I wonder about the camera. It turns out he's burnt the wires through from a distance. Shaking my head, I follow him down the hallway. I'm already regretting my decision to follow him. This is stupid. We get to the next cross passage and he repeats the same action.

'Where to now?' I ask.

'There are stairs leading upwards from here,' he says. 'They're the emergency exit.'

'How do you know?'

'You think I'm stupid? I checked them earlier.'

We enter the stairwell and I spy a camera halfway up on one of the walls. I grab Chad's arm.

'Leave this one for me.'

The cameras are on a pivot mount. I urge the air to push the camera to point at the wall. We hurry up the stairs. There's one more camera just before we reach the exit. I deal with this one too. Within minutes we're pushing on the exit door.

We step outside into the cool, clear night and look up at the sky. There are a million stars looking back down at us. Chad was an idiot for suggesting this, but I can't deny I love being out in the open again.

I take a deep breath and let it out.

Free at last.

The wind churns in the trees. Then I realize it's not the wind. It's more rhythmic than that. Like a machine. The darkness comes to life with a spotlight stabbing the ground from the sky, blinding both of us.

I realize it's attached to a helicopter.

'Put your hands up!' a voice commands from above. 'You are under arrest!'

Chapter Twenty-Four

Take my word for it. Being in jail is no fun. After being taken into custody by some thickset guards, we were handcuffed and black bags were placed over our heads. Chad tried to protest, but was cuffed about the head for his complaints.

I remained silent.

We could have fought our way out of the situation, but that would have simply made things worse. Besides, we had no desire to harm any of The Agency staff. We just wanted to have a few minutes of freedom.

After our arrest, we were taken to a cell and the bags and handcuffs were removed. The first thing Chad did after we landed in the cell was yell at the retreating backs of the guards.

'Just go to sleep,' I tell him.

Probably the worst thing about the cell was that the lights stayed on all night. The second worst thing about it was the beds. I'd thought the dorm beds were the hardest things you could possibly sleep on until we ended up in jail.

After a lot more grumbling under his breath, he does. For me, sleep does not come so easily. I dream about being in the room with Ravana. His constant questions about The Agency. Then I dream about him burning on the roof of the building as we made our escape. I see him pounding the retaining wall of the building.

Pounding and pounding and—

Someone is hitting the bars of our cell. I wake up to see Brodie on the other side. Her hair is uncombed. She looks tired and harassed. Her condition doesn't improve any upon seeing me awake.

'Do you know how long I've been standing here?' she asks.

'Ages?' I guess.

'I've been calling your name for the last ten minutes as well as hitting the bars with this cup!'

I notice she has a metal mug in her hand. 'You're kidding,' I say. 'They really give those things to prisoners?'

'What the hell do you think they drink from? Their hands?' She shakes her head in disbelief. 'What on Earth were you thinking? What made you do this?'

'That was me,' a voice comes from Chad's bunk. He blearily raises his head and regards both of us through half open eyes. 'I insisted that Mr Goody and I break out together.'

'I should have expected as much,' Brodie folds her arms. 'And can you tell me why?'

'Because I don't like to take orders!' Chad says, now fully awake and annoyed. 'I refuse to be treated like a prisoner. I'm a citizen of Norway! I shouldn't even be in the United States.'

'You're not a prisoner,' Brodie says, then realizes what she's just said. 'Well, you are now. But you weren't before.'

'I was,' he argues. 'We all are. They have no right to keep us locked up here twenty-four hours a day while they work us like animals.'

'Look,' Brodie says. 'I'm an Australian. Dan's from somewhere in China. Obviously The Agency doesn't adhere to international boundaries.'

'Or respect them!' Chad snaps.

'I know the last week has been tough,' she says.

'Really?' Chad lifts an eyebrow.

'Okay. It's been really tough. Still, we've got a mission to carry out.'

'Mission?' Chad explodes. 'I don't recall signing up for any damn mission! I want to see the paperwork!'

A guard appears at Brodie's side. 'It's time, Miss. These boys have got another visitor.'

She casts a helpless look at us. 'Don't do anything silly.'

I glance over at Chad. I don't think we can promise anything.

No sooner does Brodie leave than Twelve appears. It's the first time we've seen him since we arrived. He still doesn't look like an alien, but now he definitely resembles an ogre.

'I'm very disappointed,' he begins. 'You boys signed an agreement and now you've broken it.'

'I don't recall signing any agreements,' Chad

interrupts.

Twelve doesn't look like he often gets interrupted. 'Take my word for it. You signed an agreement and now you're going to keep to it.'

'What're you going to do?' Chad asks. 'Force us?'

'If we have to,' Twelve says quietly. 'Typhoid is not the only one able to coerce difficult subjects.'

I think back to the torture room and Ravana and his instruments. My stomach turns over at the memory. I feel light headed and dizzy as the rage builds up inside me. Without realizing it, I'm on my feet in a second.

'You will not threaten us!' I snap.

Twelve's eyes widen in surprise as his mouth becomes a thin line. 'We don't want to force you—'

'I'm out of here!' Chad interrupts. 'I'm not taking orders from some alien weirdo!'

There's a buildup of heat in the room. I see a ball of fire in Chad's hand. It grows red hot. Then white hot. Twelve steps back. To his credit he shows not a shred of fear. Chad swings around and throws the ball of fire at the wall behind us. There's an enormous explosion. Bricks and mortar fly in all directions. Even I'm showered in it.

Chad grabs my arm. 'Come on.'

Then we're running down a corridor before I know what's happening. This is all occurring so fast. Alarms start blaring. Two guards appear and I knock them over with a blast of air. We spot a couple more in another corridor and Chad blocks their passage with a block of ice.

We find ourselves in the area known as The Cavern where all the strange aircraft and equipment is stored. Personnel are running in all directions, but they obviously haven't been informed as to the nature of the threat.

We rush onto the main concourse. The easiest way out of here would appear to be up and out. I remember Doctor Sokolov telling us not to show our powers to the other personnel, but all bets are off. I point up at the doors designed to allow the aircraft to exit and focus on pushing them apart. A week ago they probably wouldn't have moved. Even now I am only able to separate them a few feet.

Through the gap I can see daylight. Grabbing Chad, we fly towards the breach. At the same time I throw a barrier up around us. I do it just in time. Someone starts shooting, but none of the bullets find their target.

We land on the grass outside the facility. Guards start appearing from the woods. They have us surrounded in seconds. All I need to do is take to the skies and I can have us out of here in seconds.

Chad grabs my arm. 'What're you waiting for? Let's move!'

I shake my head. This has all gone horribly wrong. These people may not be our friends, but neither are they our enemies.

'No,' I tell him. 'This is not right.'

'What do you mean? We need to get out of here!'

I turn to him. 'Typhoid intends to destroy a city with a nuclear weapon. Do you want to allow that to happen?'

'Well...'

'Our place is here,' I tell him firmly.

Helicopters are approaching on all sides. By now we're surrounded by about a hundred guys with machine guns. There's no doubt in my mind we could probably take them out, but I doubt we could do it without hurting people. Not without maybe killing someone. And whose side would we be on then?

I put my hands up in the air.

'Come on,' I tell Chad. 'It's time to play ball.'

Chapter Twenty-Five

It's almost a pleasure when the alarm goes off the next morning. The fluorescent light flickers into life. We shower with time to spare. We dress and make our way to the dining hall in silence.

Twelve allowed us to return to our dorm room after our surrender. I'm not sure what made him rethink his strategy. Maybe he realized he was dealing with a pair of teenage boys who could cause mayhem if we wanted. Maybe he came to the conclusion that he needed us more than we needed him.

Whatever his reasoning, we're back with the others and it feels good. Dan says nothing while he accompanies us to the dining hall. Then as Brodie and Ebony look up in surprise he jerks a thumb back at us and says, 'The jailbirds are free.'

The girls jump up and hug us both. We sit down and start eating and talking at the same time. After a while I notice Ebony goes quiet. Her face turns more pale than ever and red spots appear in her cheeks.

Chad finally notices too. 'What's wrong? Why are you looking at me like that?'

'You were just going to abandon me.' Her quiet voice is shaking with fury. 'You were going to run away and leave me.'

'No, it wasn't—'

'What else do you call it?'

'I call it fun.'

'Fun?' Her voice rises in fury.

I know Chad's the one with the ice powers, but right now Ebony is doing a great job of making the temperature drop.

She continues. 'Abandoning your sister so you can be a dork?'

'I wasn't abandoning you!'

'What sort of idiot are you? You could have gotten yourself killed. I don't—'

The argument continues till the end of breakfast. We're ready to resume training—which you may interpret as 'doing as we're told'—but it turns out there's a change in plan. Mr Brown turns up with the other trainers and leads us to a truck. We travel underground for about an hour until we reach a metal door. It groans open and instantly cold, salty air washes over us. We're looking at the ocean.

'It's a great day for the beach,' Chad comments.

Dan looks at the assembled trainers. 'Something tells me there won't be anytime for sun baking.'

Mr Brown takes the lead. 'You will be learning a new skill set today,' he explains. 'Up till now you have worked individually to hone your abilities. Today all that is going to change. Today you are going to work as a team.

'You will pass through a training mission, facing a number of obstacles until you reach the end. You will only have yourselves to rely upon.'

'Sounds tough,' Chad smirks.

Brown gives him a look. 'Today you will be facing live ammunition.' He steps up to Chad until he's only inches away from his face. 'It *will* be tough.'

He produces a map that shows our position in relation to an island. We can actually see it from where we're standing. It lies a short distance off the coast. He explains our mission. We have to get from here to the island without being detected. Then we break into a compound, and destroy an obelisk situated at the heart of the facility.

'We are throwing you in the deep end. Have no doubt about that. We are forcing you to sink or swim. We want you to think for yourselves.' He lets this sink in. 'The war game will only come to an end once your objective is achieved. You have three hours to complete your mission.'

'Uh,' Chad holds up his hand. 'What happens if we don't want to achieve our mission?'

Brown's eyes narrow. 'Say again.'

'What happens if we should decide to go for a burger and fries instead?'

Oh Chad, I groan internally.

The seconds pass slowly. A gentle morning breeze washes over the beach. A solitary seagull cries and soars away into the distance. The waves crash, race up the beach and drain into the sand.

Finally Brown's eyes move to each of us. 'If you should succeed in today's mission you will be rewarded with a twenty-four hour furlough.' He lets that thought sink in. 'If you should decide you are incapable of following orders you will be considered an enemy of The Agency and you will be treated as such.'

His eyes settle once again on Chad.

I'll say one thing for Chad. He might be a tough guy, but even he knows when he's met his match. Finally he looks to the island. 'Looks like we party tomorrow.'

Mr Brown nods and leads the other trainers back through the metal doors. He turns back one final time and looks at me.

'You remember the exercises we conducted regarding flight shapes?'

I do. 'Yes.'

'The wedge should get you to the island without being detected. It's the most like a stealth bomber. Stay low and fast.' He turns to the rest of us.

'Remember. It's *live* ammunition. You are on your own. You can die if you make a mistake.' The metal doors start to slide shut. 'Good luck.'

The doors slam shut with an ominous boom.

'Live ammunition,' Brodie says. 'Uh, where's that burger place?'

'We'll be okay,' I say, although I don't feel as confident as I sound. 'Mr Brown's right, though. We'll need to work together.'

'You're such a hero,' Chad shakes his head in mock admiration. 'Such a leader.'

I turn to him angrily. 'Is there something wrong with your brain?'

'No. Is there something wrong with yours?'

'What the hell is your problem?'

'I don't recall anyone making you leader!'

'I'm not the leader, stupid. I'm just—'

Brodie comes between us. 'Boys, switch off your glands. We need to get moving.' She checks her watch. 'We've got two hours and forty-five minutes.'

I create a wedge as Brown instructed and the others climb on. A week ago I could not have imagined building a flying device for us to fly on, but now I do it with ease. It even has a hand rail and everything. With enough practice I could probably even give it really cool fins and make the wings—

Brodie looks at me. 'Are you ready?'

I rouse myself from my dreams of becoming a flight engineer and we start across the water. It's quite an exhilarating experience. From my training with Mr Brown I know that keeping us close to the water decreases our chance of being picked up by radar. I glance over at the others. They all look so happy it's hard to believe we're heading off on a dangerous mission.

Live ammunition, I think. *Let's hope it doesn't leave one of us dead.*

Chapter Twenty-Six

We reach the island without incident. The others started studying the map on the way here. Now as we huddle in a small cave I look at the piece of laminated paper. The island is essentially a large isosceles triangle with the base at the center of the thick end. We're at the opposite end. I ask everyone what they think.

The good news is: everyone's got a plan.

The bad news is: everyone's got a *different* plan.

'We need to hit them with everything we've got,' Chad says. 'A full frontal assault where we annihilate anything that moves.'

'I think we need to creep up on the compound,' Brodie suggests. 'Then create a diversion by blowing something up.'

'We can tunnel under,' Dan says thoughtfully. 'Or leave a wooden horse out the front like they did with Troy—'

Okay, now it's getting weird.

I hold up a hand. 'There are some good ideas here. Can anyone suggest a single coordinated plan?'

No-one says anything.

Chad looks at each of us like we're stupid and marches out of the cave.

'What are you doing?' I follow him.

'You people are fools,' he says. 'I'll have this whole mission completed by the time you've worked out north from south.'

He exits from view. I shake my head in amazement.

'What is his problem?' I ask.

Ebony glares at me. 'That's my brother you're talking about.'

'Look, I didn't mean to insult him.'

She's already out of the cave. The rest of us follow her just in time to see Chad starting up the cliff face. It's an easy climb and he's most of the way up by the time we start after him. When we reach the top he's already following a trail through the thick foliage.

I get a bad feeling about this.

Why is there a trail through the undergrowth unless its—

Unless it's a trap.

At that same instant I see the wire spread out across the path.

'Chad!' I scream. 'Stop!'

He turns at the last second, but it's too late. A bolt of electricity, a blue and white jagged line of fire, arcs out of nowhere. It catches him full in the chest. The impact throws him twenty feet into the jungle.

'No!' Ebony screams.

Everyone starts forward in panic, but I'm able to stop myself. One injured person is enough. I work out the location of the generator and take it out with a single invisible ball of energy. Now it can't hurt anyone else.

Chad is motionless and pale by the time we reach him. There is a burnt, black hole scarring the middle of his chest. Brodie is checking his pulse. She looks up at me, her face filled with dismay.

'He's not breathing,' she says. 'I think he's dead.'

Under any normal circumstances any of us would produce a phone and ring for help. Unfortunately none of us own phones. Plus we have no idea as to our location.

We start CPR. Ebony presses down rhythmically on his chest as I deliver mouth to mouth. The last person on Earth I would normally want to suck face with is Chad, but right now I'm prepared to sacrifice my macho image. The minutes pass slowly. At first I think we've lost him. It's like his body has given up completely. Maybe his heart has been destroyed by the bolt of electricity. Ebony is crying. Even Dan has tears in his eyes.

How could The Agency do something like this? Have they no idea of right and wrong? Then I think of Twelve. He's not even human. If his people have been here on Earth for thousands of years, they would have seen millions of humans grow old and die.

Killing a teenager would be no big deal at all. Would it?

Then Chad groans. He reaches up blindly with

one hand and pushes me away. It takes him a few seconds to focus on the circle of faces around him. Finally he stares directly at me.

'You're damn ugly,' he says.

'I think he's going to be okay,' I tell the others.

No sooner is Chad on his feet than Ebony slaps him. The sound is like a bullet in the silent jungle.

'You are an idiot,' she says furiously.

Chad's chin quakes. For a moment I think he's going to cry. Then he dips his head. 'I'm sorry, sis. Really sorry.'

She throws her arms around him and bursts into tears. We let the family reunion continue for another minute before Brodie finally clears her throat.

'This is all very well and good, but—'

'But we've got to get going,' Chad says. 'How long was I out?'

'Too long.' Brodie checks her watch. 'We have less than two hours to reach the complex.'

'Okay,' he says, looking up at me. 'I think we

need to decide on a single plan.'

'Agreed.'

'What do you think we should do?' he asks.

It takes me a moment to realize he's asking my opinion. Maybe the electricity has jolted some sense into him. I produce the map again. Everyone had some good ideas and I think we can merge a few of them together to produce a successful strategy.

'Here's what I think we should do,' I tell them. 'We split into two groups. Group one will create a diversion at the far end of the island. Hopefully that will draw forces away from the base.

'The other group will circle around and move in from the point closest to the compound at the short end of the triangle. From there to the obelisk should only be a few hundred feet.'

'Sure,' Brodie raises an eyebrow. 'Sounds easy.'

I ignore her. 'I suggest Chad and Dan create the diversion.'

'What makes you think I'm capable of causing trouble?' Chad asks with a straight face.

I ignore him too. 'Ebony, Brodie and I will head to the compound. I think we can reach the obelisk between the three of us.'

We synchronize watches. I remind everyone that Mr Brown warned us that live ammunition is being used. Just before we part ways, I turn to Chad. 'And watch out for tripwires.'

He laughs. 'You too.'

We have an hour to make our way around the circumference of the island. It's tough going. Not only do we have to climb over the rocky coastline, but we have to watch out for traps and cameras. By the time we reach our position on the coast, we're hot and sticky in the late morning sun.

The cliff rising up from the shore is steep compared to the other sections of the island. I even wonder if it's been purpose built by The Agency to deter attacks during exercises such as this. We climb up the cliff carefully and make our way into the thick vegetation.

It looks impenetrable. It's no surprise that Chad got zapped. Any sensible person would take a path. Of course, they would almost certainly be killed, but their last moments would be spent on a pleasant trail as opposed to a hot, insect infested woodland.

'We need to hurry,' Brodie whispers.

The jungle takes another fifteen minutes to navigate. We discover three tripwires on the way. One is attached to a massive blade poised to swing down and slice the innocent victim in half.

I shake my head in disbelief when I see the device. Mr Brown wasn't kidding when he said they were using live ammunition, but surely this is a little too serious for a training exercise. What are they trying to do? Get us killed?

This is a sobering thought. I remember the warning Doctor Richards gave me about not being able to trust everyone within The Agency. Could all this just be an elaborate way to get rid of us?

No. It's ridiculous. These people actually want us to survive.

They've just got a strange way of showing it.

We push through some bushes and find a

metal fence in front of us. It's obviously not there to welcome visitors. It's about twelve feet high with barbed wire running across it at one foot intervals. My first concern is that it's electrified.

Brodie tilts her head. 'Do you hear that?'

'It's electricity.' I was right. 'We need to disconnect the power.'

'How long till Chad and Dan create the diversion?' Ebony asks.

Before I get a chance to reply, I hear a sound like a mighty wind sweeping through the forest.

I look up to see the sky falling.

Chapter Twenty-Seven

I'll say one thing for Chad.

He doesn't know the meaning of the word subtle. When I told him we needed a diversion I envisioned a fire in the jungle or a block of ice falling out of the sky. Instead, we're confronted with a full scale bombardment.

I'm not even sure *we'll* survive it.

Fire balls reign down from the sky like meteorites and slam into the ground. They seem to be landing all over the island. Some are even landing in the compound. Explosions are occurring throughout the jungle. Obviously traps are springing all over the place, detonating explosives meant to kill us. At the same time rocks are falling from the sky.

I can't work this out. Chad creates fire and ice. Dan can manipulate metals. So where are the rocks coming from?

Brodie has the answer. 'There must be a high metal content in those rocks.'

Of course.

Our ears are ringing from the multitude of explosions. So much so that I don't notice the change in the fence until Ebony grabs my arms.

'The electricity's off,' she says.

'Are you sure?'

She reaches out and grabs the fence. She doesn't turn into a barbecued chicken. Turning to me, she smiles. 'Pretty sure.'

I realize it's one of the few times I've seen her smile. She has a pretty face. Digging me in the ribs, she says, 'Will we keep moving?'

I nod. Ebony touches each of the strands of barbed wire. Each evaporates to a dry chemical within her grasp and is carried away by the wind. When there's a large enough gap, we climb through and hurry across a short distance to take refuge behind a building. From here we can easily see the obelisk. In the back of my mind I've got a vague idea to get Ebony to turn it into helium or something, but we've got to get to it first.

Two soldiers appear from around a corner.

The surprising news is they're not human.

They're some sort of battle droid. Man height. Covered in a battle suit composed of rubber and Kevlar. Armed with rifles. Before they can raise them, Brodie covers the short distance and smashes one of them in the neck. The other she flings over her left shoulder and rips its arm off.

They lay sparking and crackling in the midday sun.

Unfortunately they must have some sort of back to base alarm because a door suddenly bursts open and more of them start to pour through. I throw a boulder at them and it takes out a bunch, but this seems to cause some sort of avalanche; more start appearing from buildings all over the compound.

They start shooting and I throw up a shield. Bullets fly in all directions as we make our way through the group. Every opportunity Brodie gets, she grabs a robot and breaks him apart. Ebony turns several to gas. Finally she turns to me.

'We're almost there,' she yells above the sound of gunfire.

There's something more than a little strange in

the way she's communicated this information to me. She sounds like a chipmunk.

'Sorry,' she says. 'Helium.'

I nod.

We're only a few feet from the obelisk when the ground shakes beneath us. At first I think it's just more of the continuing barrage from Chad and Dan. Then I realize we're sinking.

'Watch out!' I yell.

The ground swallows us up in an enormous hole. We fall about twenty feet into an underground cavern. Fortunately I'm able to cushion our landing while deflecting the bullets from the battle droids above.

Brodie yells. 'Over here!'

The cave is roughly circular in dimensions, but there is a slight overhang on one side. The gunfire is relentless as we take refuge. It's only when we are out of sight that the droids stop firing. A metal ceiling slides into place. Faint lighting comes to life.

I dust off dirt from my face. I'm annoyed with myself. I should have realized there would be one final obstacle before we reached the obelisk.

'Any ideas?' Brodie asks.

'I can fly us out of here, but not until—'

'Wait a minute,' Ebony interrupts. 'We'll have to deal with them first.'

A door has slid open on the other side of the cavern. Three battle droids have appeared. They're a slightly different design to the others. Taller and more slender. I throw a row of invisible stars at them.

Nothing happens.

Damn. They must be using the same dampening field—the zeno ray—that was used against us at Ravana's building. *That's not fair! Why does this have to be so hard?*

I stop. Of course, it's not fair. This is a life or death battle designed to prepare us for…life or death.

To my surprise, Ebony is the first to move. She crosses the cavern in seconds and takes on one of the droids, hitting it with a flurry of punches. Brodie and I are close behind. I'm in immediate difficulty. My droid hits me across the face and knocks me flying. Brodie fares better. Even without her extra strength and speed, she still has her fighting knowledge. If her robot could cry uncle, I'm sure it would.

I kick the legs out from under my adversary and start hammering its head into the ground. It sweeps my legs out from under me and I land face first in the dirt. We roll around on the ground for a while. Then it straddles my body and starts punching into my face.

Despite my attempts to deflect the blows, most of them are still connecting. How long can I hold on?

The droid's head flies off and it loses power. I struggle to sit up and shake it off me. I look around. Brodie is just finishing off her droid. It's finding it hard to fight back with no arms and legs. It's Ebony who is standing before me wielding one of her arms of her droid. She is the one who has just finished her adversary and mine as well.

'How did you…what did…' I begin.

'Did you sleep through basic training?' Ebony asks. 'What was Brown teaching you?'

'How to fly. How to break the sound barrier,' I say airily. 'That sort of stuff.'

Brodie strides over just in time to see Ebony help me up. She doesn't look too happy. Not that I can blame her. Who wants to engage droids in a life and death battle of hand to hand combat?

And all before lunch?

'Where to from here?' she asks.

First we had to find the zeno emitters. It only takes a moment. They are speaker-like contraptions set into the surrounding walls. We tear them out. Then we look up at the metal ceiling. I suppose we have to get through it first. Or there's always the door the droids came through. Or maybe—

It's like Ebony can read my mind. 'Forget that. There's an easier way to get out of here.'

'How's that?' Brodie asks.

Ebony touches the wall with both hands. Closing her eyes, a tunnel appears in the rock angling up towards the surface. She stops it just before it reaches ground level. Stooping over, we climb up it until we reach the end.

'The minerals industry would love you,' Brodie says to Ebony.

The girl nods. 'I'll be a miner if the superhero gig doesn't work out.'

The ground is still shaking. Obviously Chad and Dan are still continuing their bombardment of the island. Ebony turns to me.

'What do you think is the best way to handle this?'

I shrug. 'Let's make an impact.'

Throwing a shield around us, we burst through the ground into the air. We're only a few feet from the obelisk. The droids are all standing around in silence until we make an appearance. Obviously we were out of sight and also out of mind. They start firing almost immediately. Ebony slaps a hand on the obelisk and turns it to dust.

We hover above the ground for a few seconds waiting for the droids' attack to subside.

It doesn't.

'I thought they were supposed to quit once we took out the obelisk!' Brodie yells in my ear.

I shake my head. 'I assumed the same thing too. Obviously we've still got to get off the island. I angle us across the jungle away from the compound and within minutes the droids' fire has vanished to nothing. We pick up Chad and Dan from the same place we left them. They both seem flushed with excitement.

'You should have seen it!' Dan yells as we soar across the water. 'First we were blowing up everything across the island. Then these robots appeared and we started turning them into junk.'

'Molten junk in some cases,' Chad pipes up.

Reaching the mainland I decide that we've done pretty well for ourselves. That thought is quickly put to the test, though, when I see who is waiting for us.

Twelve.

As we step onto the beach he solemnly shakes hands with each of us. Considering he probably wanted to jail us for life less than twenty-four hours ago, I'd say we've come a long way in a short time.

'It seems your mission was a complete

success,' he says.

'So now we get some time off,' Chad says, nodding.

Twelve shakes his head. 'Unfortunately not.'

'But Mr Brown said we could take a break!'

'I'm sorry,' Twelve says. 'It looks like Typhoid is preparing to move sooner than we expected. You fly out first thing tomorrow morning.' He studies each of our faces in turn.

'School's out.'

Chapter Twenty-Eight

By dinnertime we've had our wounds dressed and received a battery of shots to safeguard us against every infectious disease known to man. And then some, it seems. The burns to Chad's chest are superficial; the doctors who examine us wonder if the Alpha Project has also increased our capacity to recover from injury.

They're probably right. The gunshot wound I received when we rescued Chad and Ebony has completely healed. Sometimes it's great having super powers.

After dinner we're given a preliminary briefing of our objectives, but the main briefing will be tomorrow morning. We sit around in the entertainment room and talk about the day's events. Everyone's relaxed. Maybe part of it is pent up tension thinking about what we're about to face. Dan can't get over the shooting gallery of destruction he and Chad created. The way they describe their adventure makes it sound more like a computer game than real life.

Later Brodie and I find ourselves wandering aimlessly through one of the passageways. As we turn a corner we bump into Mr Brown.

'Ah, recruit,' he says. 'I heard you did well on the course today.' He holds out a hand. 'Congratulations.'

Amazing. Mr Brown is operating like a normal human being.

'Th-thanks,' I stammer.

'That doesn't make us brothers,' he says without a smile.

'No, I wasn't expecting—'

Then he really freaks me out. He laughs. His face breaks into a wide smile showing a wide set of teeth. Shaking his head, he says, 'If you could see your face right now…'

I'm not sure what I look like, but with Brodie watching my every move I'd rather look super cool than super geek.

'So where are you headed?' he asks.

'We were just wandering around,' Brodie

says. 'Is there any chance we could go outside?'

'I don't see why not.'

I'm amazed. Up till now this place has been like Camp X-Ray. Now all of a sudden we can just walk around like civilians. My feeling of astonishment must be reflected on my face because Brown gives me another grin and a slap on the shoulder.

'If you were going to leave you would have done it already,' he says.

Yep, I guess we would have.

He takes us up in an elevator that opens onto one of the bunkers at ground level. A large, dark field of green spreads out before us. The moon is out. The sky is clear. Brown pats my shoulder as we exit the elevator.

'Don't do anything I wouldn't do,' he says.

I don't know what he means.

Brodie just gives me a smile. We make our way across the field till we reach an embankment of rocks. We sit down and look up at the stars.

'Mr Brown seems like a nice guy, after all,' I

say.

'Didn't you think so before?'

'Are you kidding? I thought he was a monster.'

Brodie laughs. 'It's their job to train us hard.'

'Well, they're good at it.'

We sit in silence for a few minutes. I'm suddenly aware that Brodie is sitting right next to me. Very close to me, in fact. Her arm is only a few inches away. I feel my face flushing.

Should I kiss her? Does she want me to? Or would that just be weird? I don't know what to do.

She looks up at me expectantly. She's very beautiful in the moonlight. Actually, she's beautiful anytime, night or day. I imagine what could go wrong if I kiss her. She might freak out. Things might get uncomfortable and that's the last thing we want.

Tomorrow we might be facing overwhelming odds—

She kisses me. Her lips are soft against mine. She presses herself against me and I feel her heart. It seems to be beating a million miles a minute.

'What are you thinking?' she asks.

I'm in love. That's what I'm thinking, but to say it would be stupid so I just shrug.

'I don't know,' I say. 'Just thinking about tomorrow.'

'Tomorrow?' Her voice goes hard. 'What about right now?'

'Well, I was thinking—'

'Sorry,' she says, obviously miffed. 'I didn't mean to interrupt you.' She stands and smoothes her outfit.

'Hey, I didn't mean anything!'

'I know,' she flashes a quick smile at me. 'It's getting late. We should go back inside.'

I follow her back to the bunker. I feel like I've been through a tumble dryer. What did I say that was so wrong? In the elevator going down I make up my mind I'm going to kiss her goodnight. I'll do it when we reach our dorm rooms.

We walk silently through the passageways until we reach our dorms. She smiles at me like everything's fine and I try to speak.

'Brodie?'

'Yes?'

'I just wanted to say…well, you're—'

The door opens behind her. It's Ebony.

'Oh, I thought I could hear people out here,' she says. 'Sorry.'

She shuts the door. Just as it closes I hear the door behind me swing open.

'Oh, it's you guys,' Dan says. 'We're ready to turn in, Axel.'

'Yeah, sure…'

'Well, are you coming to bed?'

'I'd better go to bed too,' Brodie says.

I nod. She disappears through her door, giving me one last look before she disappears.

'Everything okay?' Dan asks.

'Peachy,' I reply.

The next morning finds us up and about at 3.00am. After a small breakfast we are led to a briefing room in another part of the complex. A man we have never met before, a guy named Hodges, brings up a display on a board. It shows a timetable with our departure time listed as 4.30am.

'I won't lie to you about this mission,' he begins. 'It's dangerous. We are taking you most of the way by plane to Cayo Placetas. About twenty miles out we'll drop you into the sea. From there you need to make your way to the island and then to the base.'

A satellite map of the island flashes up on the screen. I realize it looks very familiar.

'It's the same as the training island,' I say.

'Not exactly the same,' Mr Hodges says. 'But similar. We wanted to run you through a similar scenario before you had to face the real thing.'

'So things might be worse than yesterday?' Chad says.

'Things *will* be worse than yesterday.' Hodges turns back to the map. 'I recommend you adopt the same approach as before. Two of you create a diversion. The others make your way to the base.' He points at the map. 'This is where the missile's guidance system is stored.' He points to a cluster of buildings. The computer room is nestled in the center.

He indicates another set of buildings. 'The barracks are here...and here. Over here is the missile silo.' It is some distance from the main compound. 'As has already been explained to you, Pegasus's weakness is its dependence on its guidance system. That's what you need to take out.

'If Pegasus becomes airborne it will be almost impossible to bring down. As missiles go, it's not the fastest ever developed. In fact it's fairly slow by comparison. Its strength is its sophisticated stealth mechanism. I doubt any fighter craft could bring it down before it reaches its target.'

'Do you know what that is yet?' Brodie asks.

Hodges shakes his head. 'It's impossible to say. We have to remember this is a terrorist attack. They could aim for a smaller city like Miami or they could aim for a strategic target such as DC or New York.

'Since 9/11 New York seems to have become the preferred destination for terrorists.' He looks at each of us in turn. 'The important thing is to not let that rocket off the ground. If it takes off it will be virtually impossible to stop.'

We nod. This is all very sobering. I glance over at the others. They all look pretty serious. It's hard to believe all this responsibility is falling to us. It seems The Agency is very good at scientific research and watching the activities of humanity, but not much else.

It's almost like Hodges can read my mind. 'Your greatest advantage will be the element of surprise.'

I look at the map.

I hope the surprise is not on us.

Chapter Twenty-Nine

The plane is still high above the clouds by the time we make our jump. The man in the rear section with us is named Mr Wilkerson. He's short, red-haired and burly and goes to great lengths to tell us his experience in parachuting. Ten years with the SAS. Four years as an instructor. He's even fully trained to pilot a number of military aircraft.

'You'll be landing in the ocean, so just remember to keep your legs braced,' he says. 'And hold your breath.'

I nod. I doubt we will land in the ocean. I hope to scoop everyone together before we hit the water, but we've been told not to reveal our powers to anyone. So I just nod.

We're dressed in identical gear. They're a modified version of army fatigues. Obviously there's no insignia. I feel as anonymous now as I did when I woke up in that hotel room with the dying Doctor Richards.

We jump out one at a time into the early

morning sky. Nobody looks confident. Even Chad looks scared to death, but there's nothing any of us can do about it. As I jump, the wind catches me and I plummet towards earth. My chute opens with a jerk. Before I land I create a platform to grab everyone.

Unfortunately I miss Chad. He lands some distance from us and we collect him, sputtering and choking, from the choppy waters.

'Very clever,' he snaps.

I shrug. 'It was an accident.'

Keeping low, we make our way to the island. The sun still hasn't risen, but the sky is light. I want us to reach shore before we're too visible. We eventually find an inlet at the end of the island most distant from the base. Chad has stopped dripping by the time we climb onto the shore.

We examine our maps. We all have identical copies in case we become separated. I point out the best place for Chad and Dan to position themselves. Then we synchronize watches as we did the previous day. This time we're carrying phones to stay in contact. We set a time for two hours hence, but we will check again when we reach the base.

The lessons of the training exercise from the previous day are instantly obvious. I'm even appreciating the use of live ammunition. I dread to think how we would deal with this situation without completing a practice run.

I'm under no illusion, however, as to our lack of experience. This sort of exercise should be carried out by an elite force of armed SAS soldiers. Not a bunch of teenagers. I suppose that's the problem with The Agency. They don't like the idea of millions of people dying in a nuclear blast, but they're not prepared to do very much about it either.

The sun is just rising as we start working our way around the island. I feel terribly exposed on the shoreline, so after a few hundred feet I suggest to the girls that we move up the cliff face.

'Don't you think that'll be more dangerous?' Brodie asks.

'I think it's more dangerous to be out here where everyone can see us.'

We climb up the cliff and discover a path that

traces the coastline. I wonder if it's a trap, but then I realize the Typhoid agents need to move around Cayo Placetas as well. Still, we keep a close eye out for tripwires. We move slowly. After a few miles, Ebony grabs my arm. She urgently draws us into the undergrowth.

No sooner are we hidden than a group of four men make their way past us down the track. They are fully armed with rifles and handguns. A symbol on their jackets resembles a spider web. After a few minutes the sound of their footsteps fades.

'That was close,' Brodie whispers.

'We'd better keep moving,' I say.

We follow the path around the island. It splits into two at one point, but we keep to the trail that traces the coast. After another half hour the path starts to climb. This time I see something that makes me pause. There is a guard tower at the top of the hill. It gives a commanding view over the path and coastline.

We're stumped. Although I can't see the complex, I can hear movement and traffic coming from our right. It seems to be the obvious direction in which to head so, keeping close to the ground, we navigate through the jungle. We meet a wide muddy road cutting across through the undergrowth. It looks like it leads directly into the compound. A truck roars past us. The guards at the entry point check the back and allow it to continue through into the facility.

I begin to wonder if a more conventional form of entry might be the best method. The guard tower was constructed to watch the coast; it's out of sight from the complex. No-one is watching the tops of the vehicles. When the next truck heads past us towards the compound, I propel us softly onto the roof. The vehicle pauses for what seems an eternity at the gate. The men talk about a new shipment of arms. Then it continues on into the facility.

I can see it's heading towards a warehouse, so we jump free and roll under the nearest building. There are guards everywhere. I'm not too sure how successful we'll be at staying hidden. It only seems a matter of time before we're discovered.

Pulling out the map, we work out our current location. The computer room is still some distance away; at least a few hundred feet. It's a shame it's daylight. This might have been easier at night.

'Take us up to the roof,' Ebony whispers. 'Then we can hop from building to building.'

That seems like a good idea. I wait until some guards wander past then fly us up and onto the roof. We flatten ourselves against the flat metal and slide quietly along the top until we reach the end. I fly us across to the next building and repeat the process two more times.

I start to feel hopeful.

With a lot of luck this might work. A large building lies before us. Checking our map again I work out that this is the computer complex. I glance over the edge of the roof and spy two guards at the front door. Obviously we're not entering through there.

I look at my watch. We still have a few minutes before Chad and Dan are due to create their diversion. At any rate we need to check in to confirm the time. I watch a truck weave its way through the jungle down the muddy road to the front gate. A guard jumps out and speaks to the gatekeeper. They both look in the back. One of them waves the truck through into the compound.

I don't know why, but my heart is beating faster. This doesn't look good. The truck draws to a halt and they open up the back. More men race up to the vehicle and climb into the rear.

When they exit, they're carrying two bodies.

It's Chad and Dan.

Chapter Thirty

Ebony stifles a cry. Brodie looks shocked. Even I can't quite assimilate this latest piece of information. Chad and Dan have been captured. This was not mentioned in any scenario we planned.

We need to get them back, but it's more important we take out the computer first.

'I've got an idea,' I tell the girls.

A few minutes later Ebony reduces a sheet of the metal roofing to oxygen, exposing the recess in the roof. Climbing in, we find ourselves among air conditioning ducts and cross beams. The ceiling beneath our feet seems to be made of timber. As long as we move quietly we should remain undetected.

We make our way across the roof. I get Ebony to create a coin sized hole and I peer down through it to the room below. It takes me a moment to get my bearings. I can see men moving around a large chamber. A computer terminal sits in the center. A man seems to be adjusting dials.

This must be the missile computer. I'm just

about to get Ebony to create an even bigger hole when she grips my shoulder.

'We can't go down there yet,' she says.

'What do you mean?'

'We have to save Chad and Dan.'

I shake my head. 'Stopping the missile is more important.'

'After they know we're here it will be impossible to save the boys.' She lets this information settle. 'Let me go back and get them.'

'We've got to take out the computer!'

'Give me fifteen minutes. That's all I ask.'

I look at Brodie. She says, 'Ebony's right. Once Typhoid knows we're here it will be impossible to save Dan and Chad.'

I slowly nod. Once they know the building's under attack they'll try to hold Dan and Chad as hostages. Or worse, they'll simply kill them.

'You've got fifteen minutes.' We check our watches. 'I can't give you any longer. There's too much riding on this.'

She makes her way across the roof and

disappears from sight. I turn my gaze to Brodie. It's uncomfortably close in here. My mind floats back to the previous night. I want to speak to her about it, but now is not the time.

The minutes tick by slowly. Eventually I'm ticking off the seconds. Sixty seconds. Forty-five seconds. Finally we're out of time.

'We've got to do this,' I say.

Brodie nods glumly.

The ground shakes as if there's an earthquake. A resounding explosion rocks the camp.

What the—?

Grabbing my arm, Brodie hisses, 'That's our cue!'

I had intended using Ebony to dissolve the roof under us. Instead I drive a force field straight into it. It collapses under us and we rapidly drop to the floor below. We have the element of surprise, but only for a few seconds. Scientists are staring at us in astonishment. Even the guards look amazed.

Then one of them yells, 'Shoot them!'

The bullets start to fly. I throw up a shield and

the bullets rebound off it in all directions. One of them hits a scientist in the head, killing him instantly. At the same time Brodie grabs one of the guards, breaks his arm and uses him as a shield as another guard opens fire.

The man is dead, but then Brodie grabs his weapon and strafes the chamber with gunfire.

'The computer!' she yells.

Keeping my shield in position, I build up my concentration.

Now, I tell myself. Now. Now.

Now!

I throw a blast of air as powerful as a small tornado at the computer and it explodes into a thousand pieces of jagged metal. The debris flies in all directions. Some of it even tears straight through the walls, creating serrated holes through which we can see daylight.

Yes!

Now for the others. Not that Brodie really needs my help. In a matter of seconds we've created a scene of utter mayhem. Men are dying all over the place. I remember a few days ago I had reservations about taking a human life. It saddens me to think about how casual it all now seems.

But it has to be done. It's them or us. It's war.

I sweep a group of men towards a wall and they're knocked out or killed immediately. We head towards a door. We've got to find the others and get out of here. I demolish the door—indeed, the whole side of the building—with one blast of air. In the clearing beyond there are guards racing towards us firing madly.

Thank God for the shield.

We would be mincemeat without it. Now we have to find the others. I suddenly remember seeing a building on the map that Hodges marked as a storage block. Why didn't I think of this before?

I angle Brodie and myself between two buildings while I pick up debris and hurl it at the approaching troops.

'Do you know where we're going?' she yells.

'I think so.' We approach a brick building and I try building up enough focus to punch a hole in the side of it. My efforts don't work. I can't concentrate. I'm already deflecting bullets and hurling as much debris at these guys as I can.

'I can't open the door!' I cry.

Brodie darts forward and grabs the door handle. It swings opens easily.

'You ever heard of one of these?' she asks.

I follow her inside. The interior of the building is far quieter than I expected. The walls must be reinforced. No wonder I couldn't break in. We follow a narrow corridor to the end. I make the mistake of momentarily dropping my shield. As we turn the corner we are confronted by an artillery gun.

It's aimed right at us.

I throw up my shield as it fires its mortar. It hits my shield, but the blast is so powerful it still permeates the barrier. We both hit the floor—hard. Lifting my head, I check on Brodie. I'm relieved to see her staggering to her feet.

'What hit us?' she asks.

'Something big,' I tell her.

The artillery gun is set to fire automatically.

Beyond it lies another metal door. This building is proving to be something of a Chinese puzzle box. No sooner do you infiltrate one level than you are confronted by another. A small slit allows access to the room beyond.

Brodie peers through it. 'I can see them! They're on the floor! They've got Ebony too!'

'Stand back.'

I build up a blast of air. I'd like to say it tears the door off its hinges, but my focus is completely haywire now. The door sort of flies off and slides to the floor. We enter the room beyond and check their pulses.

'They're unconscious,' Brodie says. 'I think they've been drugged.'

Something about this doesn't make sense. I can't initially work out what it is. Then realization hits me. My stomach churns over uncomfortably.

If Chad, Dan and Ebony were all captured and knocked out, then who was causing all the explosions?

It's almost as if we've been drawn here on

purpose...

The answer comes to me in a flash.

'It's a trap!' I yell. 'We've got to get out!'

But the gas is already pouring from the ceiling. I'm supposed to be a master of air, but now I can't get enough of it to even sustain myself.

Within seconds the floor rushes up to meet me.

Chapter Thirty-One

My eyes slowly open.

The first thing I hear is Chad.

Why does it have to be Chad?

'Looks like sleeping beauty is awake,' he comments.

It takes a moment to focus, but it makes me wish I had stayed asleep. Nothing I see bodes well for the future. We are in an enclosed cell. It appears to be the same type of cell that held Ebony and Chad back in Ravana's building. A mesh of wire covers the front. Each of us is chained to the rear wall with metal cuffs over our heads. The strain in my arms is terrible. My feet reach the floor, but just barely.

I know it's pointless trying my powers, but I do anyway.

Nothing.

'Don't bother trying your powers,' Brodie says. 'They're using those zeno ray emitters.'

'I would have already burnt their faces off,' Chad advises me. 'If I could.'

I glare at him. 'What happened to you guys, anyway? You were supposed to create a diversion.'

Chad looks away. 'We were…uh, overtaken by superior numbers.'

'They shot us with that stun ray,' Dan says. 'We were busy skipping stones.'

At first I think I've misheard him. 'Skipping stones? You must be joking.'

If looks could kill, Chad's glare at Dan would strike him cold dead. 'Did you have to tell Mr Goody Two-Shoes?'

I'm about to explode at Chad, but at that moment the door to the room swings open and a man in a Typhoid uniform enters. He is tall, European looking with stark white hair. He does not look very old, so his hair must have aged prematurely. He is wearing gloves. Two guards flank him.

'So the children have awoken,' he says. 'Good. We must keep moving. Time is money as they say.'

'Who are you?' Chad asks. 'Let us out of here!'

The man makes a tut-tutting sound as he shakes his head. 'You are not the one giving orders here, boy. I am. I will be the one who decides who lives and who dies and when that will happen.'

Well, if there's such a thing as a conversation killer, that's it.

'I am General Solomon Wolff,' he says. 'I was not born with that name, but it is the name by which I am now known. You know a little about me and my organization and I, in turn, know a little about you.'

He pauses, but none of us say anything.

'Now you are silent. Later you will speak. You will beg to make yourselves heard. Some of you have already been introduced to one of our 'motivational' devices. We have many others. If you thought you previously experienced pain, I assure you it is only a taste of what we can dispense.

'As I say, I know a little about you. I know about The Agency and its alien representatives. I know about their eternal watching and the scientists that work with them. Perhaps you do not know that there are other aliens here on Earth. They also have their affiliations and their aspirations for our planet.'

None of us say anything to this.

'By creating you—a super powered mercenary—The Agency has created an imbalance in the power structure of the world,' Wolff says. 'There are governments that will pay handsomely to have that balance redressed.'

'What do you want from us?' I ask.

'First there will be blood.' He pretends to look shocked. 'Oh no. We are not so inhuman that we intend to beat you bloody. No, we want your blood to examine. If it is possible to replicate the processes that created you, then we can make you in our own form.

'What could be better than to create an army of super beings? Nothing could stop such an army. It would be invincible.'

'Funny,' Brodie says. 'I think Hitler had similar ideas and see what a loser he was.'

'You compare me to Hitler,' Wolff shakes his head. 'I have no such grandiose ideals. Money is power. It is a simple ingredient to life that oils the wheels of the world and makes all things possible.'

The door to the room opens again and a figure enters. My blood runs cold. The man looks like a mummy. His entire body is covered in bandages.

Wolff chuckles. 'I believe you know the good Doctor Ravana? His appearance has changed somewhat since your last encounter.'

Ravana yells a command and two guards enter the chamber and unlock the cell. They go straight to Ebony.

'No!' Chad screams. 'Leave her alone.'

Ravana enters the cell and punches Chad hard in the stomach. Once. Twice. Three times.

As Chad hangs helplessly from the wall, struggling to regain his breath, Ravana grasps his head with a bandaged hand.

'You are the fire boy who set me alight,' Doctor Ravana says. 'I will save something special for your interrogation.'

The doctor turns his attention to Ebony and injects her with a needle. Within seconds her eyes roll up into her head and she sags from the wall. The guards unchain her and drag her from the room.

'You bastard!' Chad gasps. 'Leave my sister alone!'

'She is not alone,' the general says as he relocks the cell. 'Doctor Ravana will be keeping her company.' He makes his way to the door. 'One final thing. The Agency seemed to believe that Pegasus operated under a separate guidance system. I assure you nothing could be further from the truth. We rectified that weakness when we modified the missile. Pegasus is fully capable of finding its way to New York on its own.

'We are making history within the hour. It is a shame you will not be present for the launch.' He pauses. 'What is it you American's say? Adios?'

The general exits the room.

Brodie mutters under her breath, 'I'm not American.'

The only other sound is Chad trying to regain his breath.

'Can anyone use their powers?' I ask. 'At all?'

'Not me,' Dan says.

'Me neither,' Brodie answers.

'Chad?' I ask.

He simply shakes his head. I can't believe that things have turned out so badly. Not only have we been captured, but destroying the computer system did nothing to delay the launch of the rocket. And it appears New York is the target. The same streets we were walking on a few days ago are about to turn to rubble and molten metal.

And the people—

'But I do have a plan,' Brodie says.

'What is it?' I ask.

'You seem to have forgotten I'm a whiz with locks,' Brodie says. She slips off her boots with her toes and pulls out a long piece of metal. Within seconds she's gripping it between her toes and has swung up so the metal is inserted into my cuffs.

'You've got to be joking,' I say.

'Do you want to be free?'

About a minute later I hear a satisfying click and the cuff comes loose. I try unlocking Brodie's cuffs, but even with her detailed instructions it still takes about ten minutes. Once she's free, the others are loose in moments.

'How did you learn to do all that?' Chad asks.

'Beats me,' Brodie says. 'It's all part of my previous life. Whatever that was.'

'There's just one problem,' I tell them.

We turn to look at the wall of the cell. It is only composed of vertical bars covered by a metal mesh, but without our powers it may as well be solid concrete.

Chapter Thirty-Two

'You're right,' Chad says. 'That is a problem.'

The zeno emitters are suspended from the opposite walls like spot lights. Obviously they're responsible for stripping us of our powers. Possibly we would only need to be a short distance from the cell and our powers would return to normal. I glare at the devices. It's only a couple of feet, but it might as well be miles.

Chad glances down at Dan. 'You're pretty skinny.'

'Thanks,' he says. 'I think.'

'No, I mean you might be able to fit your arm through the wire.'

He looks askance at the diamond gaps between the metal mesh. They're *very* small. 'And then what?'

I see what Chad is suggesting. 'If you can reach far enough through the wire you might be able to get your powers to activate in your arm.'

'In my arm?' Dan is looking at us like we've

grown extra heads. 'So I'll have a super-arm. Are you kidding?'

'It's worth a try,' Brodie urges. 'Come on. Stick your arm through.'

To Dan's credit, he wrestles his fist through the gap and pushes his arm through as far as it will go.

'It won't go any further,' he says.

'Try breaking the wire,' I suggest to him.

'With what? I don't have any pliers.'

'With your mind, of course!'

'Don't yell at me!'

'I'm not yelling,' I say, lowering my voice. 'You've got to push your arm out further.'

He reaches out further.

'Now try to bend the mesh,' Chad suggests.

'I am trying. Nothing's happening.'

'Try harder.'

'I am. My arm is stuck.'

'You need to go out further—' I start.

'Angle to the left—' Chad urges.

'I can't reach it.' Dan is almost in tears, 'My

arm won't reach far enough.'

'Wait a minute.' Brodie holds up the lock pick. 'Try holding onto this.'

'Why?' Dan asks. 'For good luck?'

'No! You might be able to use it like an antenna.'

'So now I'm a human antenna!' Dan groans, but grabs the piece of metal from her and pushes his arm back through the wire.

'Further,' Chad urges.

'Shut up,' he grunts.

'Just a bit further!'

'Shut up!' He says furiously.

He pushes his arm through the gap with all his might and I can see scratches all the way up his arm where it has rubbed against the wire. Tears of frustration fill his eyes. The piece of metal dangles precariously from the end of his fingertips.

A sound comes from the wall. I look up. One of the emitters on the wall is moving. It is shaking.

'It's working,' I say quietly. 'You've got to keep going.'

The emitter continues to jiggle as if an earthquake is shaking the room. I see perspiration break out on Dan's forehead as his eyes focus on the emitter. A line of sweat seeps down his temple. Tears trickle across his cheeks. The emitter wobbles from side to side. It breaks free from the wall, a single wire holding it in position.

It snaps free and clatters to the floor.

The door to the room flies open and a guard races in. He raises his gun. At the same moment, Dan clenches his fist and the door to our cell flies off its hinges and slams into the guard, knocking him unconscious. We exit the enclosure and make our way into the hallway outside.

'Well done,' I slap Dan on the shoulder.

'Yeah,' Chad says grudgingly. 'Pretty good for a kid.'

'For a kid!' Dan snaps.

Chad ruffles his hair. 'Stay cool, shorty.'

We hurry down the hallway. Before long we've arrived at another room. Chad pushes the door open and we all stop in the doorway. Ebony is chained to the table. Ravana is sitting across from her. He is motionless. And where his skin is showing through the bandages is white. Very white.

Ebony has turned him to salt.

She is not wearing one of her shoes. 'I touched him with my foot,' Ebony says with anguish. 'He was going to hurt me again.'

Chad embraces her as I remove her restraints with my mind. 'It's okay, sis,' he says. 'You did what you had to do.'

He'll get no argument from me.

We hasten from the building and race through the camp to the exit. Some sort of evacuation seems to be taking place, so the guards are hurrying in all directions. Now that the missile is ready for firing they must be preparing to withdraw from the island.

'We need to stop that weapon,' I say.

'We also need to dish out some payback,' Chad replies grimly.

Before I can say a word he releases Ebony and reaches out with clenched fists. A group of soldiers notice us for the first time. He sends balls of fire barreling towards them. As they are blasted backwards, he turns to us.

'Find the missile,' he says. 'I'll keep the rest of them busy.'

We head through the gates of the camp. Other soldiers start firing at us, but I fling them aside and we continue down the road. I remember the turn in the path I noticed earlier. Behind us I can hear a multitude of explosions. The sound of fire fills the air. Chad is obviously having fun back there. I hope he's okay.

The jungle embraces us. We are moving quickly down the path, but we still have to watch for traps.

Finally we reach a clearing. A concrete bunker is located to one side. I see a figure break from the jungle and race towards it.

General Wolff.

'Stop!' I yell.

We hurry towards the bunker as he disappears inside. The building appears to be made from reinforced concrete. I struggle to break through, but it is too thick to tear apart.

'Dan, I need your help.'

Together we focus on the metal entry door. I find it almost impossible to budge. Slowly it starts to bend outwards from its hinges.

'It might be made of iridium,' Ebony says. 'That's one of the strongest metals known to man.'

Finally we tear the door from its housing. I expect to face a hail of bullets, but instead General Wolff steps confidently from the interior of the bunker. He looks like he could have just turned up for a garden party.

'You children are most resourceful,' he says. 'Unfortunately, you are too late.'

The ground shudders under us. I turn to see the missile rising up from the jungle behind us.

'The missile is on its way,' Solomon Wolff says. 'And nothing can stop it.'

Chapter Thirty-Three

I turn to the others. 'I've got to try.'

'We'll look after him,' Brodie says and follows up with a punch to the mercenary's jaw. He crumples into a heap.

Then I'm off the ground and into the air. The missile is already high above the island and moving away faster with every second. I look back down at Cayo Placetas and see the others grouped around Wolff's inert body. This might be the last time I see them.

I'm going to bring down Pegasus or die trying.

The missile continues straight up into the sky. I pursue it. The air becomes colder. It seems to fight against me and I have to remind myself it's supposed to be my friend. I flatten myself into as streamlined a shape as possible as Mr Brown showed me. I'm going to need every advantage I can get if I'm going to stand a chance.

Up ahead of me I see the tiny body of the missile against the indigo blue sky. Pegasus is long and thin with vents to allow the intake of air. Like any jet engine, it compresses the air and ignites it, forcing itself through the sky; a controlled explosion that drives it forward on a column of thrust.

Pegasus continues to rise, but slowly its rate of ascent becomes an arc. It is aiming towards it target now. New York City. I try to cut across its arc slightly, grow slightly closer, but now it puts on an extra burst of speed.

The sky before me explodes. Shielding my eyes, at first I think Pegasus has erupted in mid flight. Then I realize the explosion has come from somewhere else. A fighter plane appears in my peripheral vision. It has fired on the missile. Its rocket has come close, but the missile has nimbly changed course to avoid it.

The fighter plane fires again. This time I actually watch its projectile streak through the sky. Just as it seems destined to strike Pegasus, the missile jerks about crazily and the projectile explodes.

It takes a few seconds for me to realize what I have just witnessed. I know a technique often used by fighter craft is to release chaff as a decoy to mislead attacking fire. This is exactly what the missile has done.

At the same time I see something arcing back across the sky towards the fighter plane. It doesn't seem possible. It's a tiny dot of black, no more than a full stop embedded in the blue page of sky.

The fighter craft explodes into a fiery ball.

I feel the color drain from my face. Pegasus is more than a missile. It is a fully equipped battle system. Not only can it avoid oncoming attacks, but it can fight back as well.

Might have been nice of Twelve to mention this.

The missile changes direction again.

I glance down. We are high above the ocean. We're still far from land, but I know we're probably charging directly towards Florida. The missile may curve inland or may follow the long coast towards New York. It can move at almost three times the speed of sound so it will take less than an hour to reach its target. I need to speed up if I intend to stand any chance of catching up with Pegasus.

But how can I move that fast?

The fastest I traveled in training was little more than twice the speed of sound and even that was simply in a straight line. A memory comes back to me from Mr Brown. He spoke about how I might be able to increase my speed if I could create a vacuum directly ahead of me. Such an action would be impossible for a normal fighter jet—they need air to function—but it was theoretically possible for me because of my ability to control air.

Theoretically possible.

It's not much, but it's all I've got.

I pour on more speed. At the same time I focus on dispersing the air directly before my flight path. After a few seconds I realize Pegasus is closer. Or rather, I've grown closer to it.

How long do we have? We've been in the air almost half an hour. The wind is tearing past me and now it's increasingly hard to breathe. I'm not sure how long I can keep going like this, but at least now I'm making some headway. The missile is now less than a mile away.

Something catches my eye. Three somethings. I glance over and see a series of fighter craft winging through the sky towards the missile. At the same time I see them fire and rockets arch across the sky towards Pegasus. Once again I see tiny dots leave the rear of Pegasus just before the rockets strike.

The projectiles explode in mid flight.

Simultaneously, three rockets eject from Pegasus and head towards the fighter craft. They take evasive maneuvers, rolling and somersaulting through the sky. One of them is struck almost immediately. The second fighter executes a quick roll and fires two more shots at the missile.

As Pegasus disposes of the two rockets I see the second fighter craft burst into flame. It draws a long blackened stain across the sky before disappearing from sight.

Now it's only me and a single fighter craft remaining. So far the lone ship has avoided Pegasus' retaliatory action. As this realization sinks in I catch sight of something that chills me to the bone. I've been so intent on keeping up with Pegasus that I haven't noticed the changing landscape below. I can see a section of coast. It's the distinctive shape of Chesapeake Bay. New York is only minutes away.

Time is running out.

I pour on even more speed, but the missile seems to be capable of going even faster. It jerks suddenly in the sky and another missile explodes, but still it remains aloft. It can be only seconds before it detonates.

Something explodes near me and the blast throws me off course.

No!

I veer out of control for a few seconds, cartwheeling through the sky like a firework. *Where is Pegasus?* I spy a tiny silver streak in the sky. It seems to be reducing altitude. It must be preparing to detonate. I aim towards it, pouring on as much speed as I can. The shockwave from the blast has slowed me down and now I've got to make up for lost time.

I can see Long Beach and a main road. It must be the Garden State Parkway. Eventually it meets up with the New Jersey Turnpike. New York is only moments away. I either stop the missile now or I never will. I give a final burst of speed and see the remaining fighter craft fire three more rockets at the missile. They explode impotently in mid air. Even I think the fighter's efforts are fruitless.

Now the jet aircraft pours on more speed. I think I realize what the pilot intends to do. If he can't shoot the missile down he intends to set a collision course with the weapon. He understands the stakes as well as me.

Even then I doubt he will succeed. The designers of Pegasus took into account the capabilities of the greatest fighter craft in the world. They knew exactly what to expect.

Of course, they didn't know about me.

They didn't know that one day a teenage boy would be turned into some sort of super weapon.

A super hero.

And now I know what I have to do.

Pegasus is just like any other jet engine. It requires an intake of air to propel it forward. There's no time left to wonder if this is going to work. There's only time to act because *millions of people are about to die.*

Instead of projecting a vacuum ahead of myself, I project it around the body of Pegasus. The effect is almost instantaneous. The missile seems to stutter in mid flight. Its jet engines can't operate without air.

Something whirrs past me at incredible speed. The remaining fighter pilot has realized something is wrong with the missile. He has gotten off a shot in the hope it may impact.

A bright flash appears before me. I close my eyes, expecting the worse. Has the warhead exploded? Has the city dissolved in molten destruction? Have a million people lost their lives in a hellfire of nuclear energy?

I slowly open my eyes.

Chapter Thirty-Four

'Congratulations.' Twelve shakes my hand. 'Congratulations on a job well done.'

I realize it's the first time I have actually touched the alien. He feels surprisingly human. He gives me a final nod and moves on to shake hands with a very surprised looking Dan.

It's a party and God knows I don't remember ever having celebrated another party. I don't remember birthdays or Christmases or christenings or anything else so I intend to make the most of this one.

Three days have passed since the destruction of Pegasus. Our role in the attack on Typhoid and the destruction of the rocket are still a secret to most of the personnel at The Agency. There are a hundred projects taking place here at any one time and our efforts to save New York City just happen to be one of them.

Brodie sidles up to me. 'Looks like we're suddenly Twelve's best friends.'

'I think whoever gets the job done is his best

friend,' I tell her quietly. 'Anyway, the operation wasn't a complete success.'

I suppose I'm being hard on myself. Typhoid was not finished, but Mr Jones informed us the organization had been dealt a severe blow; Solomon Wolff was now on the run. Where he would turn up next was anyone's guess.

So Typhoid was down, but not out as was Wolff. That's a disappointment. I would have liked to have seen Solomon Wolff languishing in a cell considering everything he wanted to put us through.

Still…

'Stop brooding,' Brodie nudges me. 'You saved New York City from certain destruction.'

'Me and another guy. A fighter pilot I never got to thank.'

She presses my arm. 'The world is made up of nameless heroes.'

Someone appears at my side. Doctor Sokolov.

I give her a smile. 'Come to join the party?'

She returns the smile, but I can sense a strain playing behind the curve of her mouth. 'I thought I would add my congratulations to the all conquering heroes.' Her eyes shift to Brodie and across to Twelve. She takes my arm. 'Have you tried the canapés?'

The Doctor gently leads me over to the table. I fire a glance at Brodie. I don't know if she looks troubled or just plain jealous. It's hard to tell with that girl. The doctor passes me a paper plate. On it sits a cracker decorated with cream cheese and chicken breast.

'These are very good,' she says, her eyes boring into mine. 'But you must be careful not to eat them too quickly.'

She smiles and looks over my shoulder with a look of delight. 'Harry! I didn't expect you here today!'

Disappearing into the crowd, I'm left standing there with the paper plate and the single savory. Brodie comes over.

'What was that all about?'

I shrug. 'Oh, nothing. She just likes her food. That's all.'

I hate to lie to Brodie. If there's anyone I've come to trust, it's her. I would—and already have—entrusted my life to her a dozen times over. Still, someone told me something a lifetime ago that has kept me alive till now.

Trust no-one.

I make some more small talk before gently extricating myself from the party and into the gentleman's toilet. I step into one of the cubicles and pull the savory from my pocket. In the center of it is a folded piece of paper.

On it is written:

Corridor 11E / 16:00 hours

Nothing else.

She's a woman of few words, I think.

I'm trying to make light of the whole incident, but my stomach knows better.

There's something seriously wrong here. When I first woke up in that room, Doctor Richards told me I should seek out The Agency. But what did he say?

'Some…at The Agency…will help you.'

Some at The Agency are on our side. What about the others? Are they our enemy? Who here can be trusted?

Can I can trust Doctor Sokolov? How do I know she's not some sort of double agent?

My mind whirls in confusion. I stand in the cubicle mulling over my options. In the end I realize there's only one thing I can do. I have to meet with her. At least I have my powers. I will be on guard the whole time. If she tries to take me down, if it looks like it's any sort of trap—

Well, I just took down a missile. I think I can handle a solitary scientist.

The next few hours pass slowly. Chad and Dan want me to join them above ground to toss a ball around, but I tell them I'm busy. I mope around our dorm room until the time draws near. Then I make my way to the junction indicated on the note. When I arrive I realize this point has been chosen for a very specific reason. It is one of the few areas not monitored by security cameras.

No sooner have I found the spot than a nearby

door opens slightly. I can just make out Anna's figure in the doorway.

'Quickly,' she says.

She urges me through the door, securing it behind me. I find myself in a narrow corridor. The silence closes in around me.

'You must follow me,' Anna says. 'We will be missed if we are gone for too long.'

'What is this about?' I demand. 'I'm not going anywhere.'

She grips my arm. 'Listen! You and your friends are in terrible danger! If you want to survive you must come with me.'

That's a hard argument to ignore. I follow her down the corridor. It quickly becomes obvious that this is not one of the regular passageways used by Agency personnel. It is more like a service tunnel used for telecommunications and plumbing. Pipes and air conditioning ducts line the ceiling. The lighting is non-existent in some places. I half expect someone to leap out of the shadows at me.

Finally Anna stops before a manhole in the

floor. She lifts it up, reaches into the gap and flicks a switch. A weak, electric light illuminates a ladder below.

'We must go down here,' she says.

I shake my head. 'Not until I find out what is going on. I've followed you this far, but how do I know you're not trying to kill me?'

'You silly boy.' Anna rolls her eyes. 'I am trying to save your life. As did Doctor Richards and the other members of the Alpha Project.'

'You mean when Typhoid attacked The Agency?'

Anna starts down the ladder. 'Typhoid did not attack The Agency.' She stops to look up at me. 'He and the other scientists were trying to save you from it.'

Chapter Thirty-Five

I follow Anna down the ladder. The corridor below is old. Almost ancient. It curves around in a wide bend. The ground underfoot is rough. It feels like we've walked miles. Every six feet there is another feeble light set into the ceiling. Anna turns into another corridor. A feeble light shines at the end.

'This tunnel was originally built during the Civil War. It was used to store ammunition and supplies. Later The Agency constructed its base over it. Very few people even within The Agency know of these tunnels.'

'I don't care about your tunnels,' I say. 'What is going on? What does The Agency intend to do?'

'It's not what they intend to do.' Anna draws to a halt. 'It's what they've already done.

'Doctor Richards was the lead scientist involved in the Alpha Project. He was able to convince many of the others that what they were doing was wrong. They transported you out of here despite knowing it would probably cost them their lives.' Anna unlocks an ancient door and pushes it wide open. 'But he was not able to get everyone out.'

My heart is pounding as I enter the room. It's barely six feet by eight feet. It contains a kid, maybe thirteen years old with thin black hair, sitting on a bunk located close to the floor. He is wearing a t-shirt and shorts. His shoes are too large for him. On his arms are needle marks, but they are so faint they're almost invisible. Hanging from the ceiling is a single light bulb suspended from a chain. There is a small hand basin and toilet. At the other end of the chamber is a second door similar to the first. Iron bars in the grate look out onto blackness.

At first I think the paint on the walls is peeling, but then I realize the dark, tight patches are writing. Words. Formula. Languages. Lines and lines of information cover every inch of the cell.

The kid looks up without seeing me. It's like he's looking through me. My throat is dry. I think if I try to make a sound it will come out as a whisper. My legs are shaking so hard I can hardly stand.

I lean against one of the walls for support.

How could this be allowed to happen?

'This is Ferdy,' Anna says.

'Mr Jones said they tried to make the procedure work with adults.'

'There were other children before you,' Anna nods. 'Many of them. Some of them were sent away to other facilities. Most did not survive the process. Ferdy is the last one of the previous batch who—'

'Batch?' I can hear my voice rising. 'You make him sound like an experiment.'

Tears fill the doctor's eyes. She wrings her hands together. 'We did not know it would be like this. I swear it. We thought we would be experimenting with animals. It was only after we started that I realized we were using human subjects.'

'You should have refused!'

'Refused?' Anna looks at me in disbelief. 'It's impossible to refuse Twelve. Other aliens who work within The Agency are not like him. But as far as Twelve is concerned, you are either with him or against him. He rules with an iron fist. Most of the scientists who work within The Agency do not suspect the breadth of its experiments.'

I turn to the figure sitting on the bed. 'Ferdy. Are you alright?'

He remains silent.

'Ferdy?' I try again. 'Can you hear me?'

'The area of a triangle.' He stops. 'The area is calculated my multiplying half the base times the height.'

I'm not sure what to make of this. 'Okay.' I continue. 'My name is Axel. I'm here to help you. We're going to leave this place. Do you understand what I'm saying?'

He looks through me again. 'The highest mountain is on Mars. It is Olympus Mons and rises to a height of 69,459 feet.' He stops. 'And yes, Ferdy understands you.'

I nod in relief. 'I am a friend.'

'The most abundant element in the universe is hydrogen,' he tells me.

'He has a photographic memory,' Anna explains.

'Has he always been like this?'

She shakes her head. 'No. He was a perfectly healthy little boy when he arrived. It was only after the experiments that he changed as did all the others. They changed or they perished.'

'Are these experiments still being carried out?'

'Not now. Doctor Richards destroyed all the research before he ran away with you and the others. Twelve has been trying to get me to reproduce Richard's work, but it's impossible.' Anna's face looks so yellow in the pale light she appears unwell. 'I swear I didn't know it would be like this.'

'Sacrifices must always be made for the greater good,' a voice says from behind us.

We spin around. Twelve has a gun pointed directly at Anna.

He pulls the trigger.

Chapter Thirty-Six

I'm not fast enough.

If I were faster I could have thrown up a barrier, but because I'm not—

The bullet hits her.

Anna rebounds against the wall. She tries to stay on her feet, but gravity drags her to the floor. At the same time Twelve disappears from the doorway and the sound of his footsteps recede up the narrow corridor. I kneel next to Anna, taking her hand. I am reminded of when I woke up in the hotel room with Doctor Richards on the floor. History is repeating itself.

Ferdy's small hand touches Anna's forehead as she tries to speak.

'The average resting pulse of a human is sixty to ninety beats per minute,' he says softly. 'Doctor Anna is a friend.'

I try to staunch the bleeding. 'Anna. I'll get help.'

But no sooner are the words out of my mouth

than a blast erupts down the passageway behind us. I instantly throw up a shield to protect us from the worst of it. Dust flies everywhere. Cracks appear in the walls. The lights go out and for a long moment I think the whole structure is about to cave in around us.

Finally the noise subsides and we're left in complete and total darkness. No matter what my powers may be, there's no way I can navigate out of a black hole a hundred feet underground.

The light bulb flickers back on. Faintly. I stare at it, daring it to die out.

It fades once, but returns to life, casting a faint yellow glow around the cell.

I'm still trying to stop the blood flow from Anna's chest, but it's like trying to plug a hole in a dam with a pebble. I look down into her face. She is pale. She's lost a lot of blood. I'm not sure even a doctor could save her.

'You have to escape The Agency,' she urges. 'It's…'

'Just hold on. I'll get us…'

'It's too late for me. Take Ferdy.' She swallows hard as a spasm of pain works through her body. 'We didn't know…the children…wrong, but I never realized…'

'Anna…'

Her eyes open wide. 'You should know…you have…'

She struggles to speak.

'…a brother…'

The silence closes in around us. Ferdy strokes her face, murmuring details about chemical compounds and how Anna was his friend. This is how it all started. A small room. A dying person. Enigmatic words.

I have a brother.

I shake my head. Now is not the time to think about such things. I'm not sure how much air we have left remaining in this small chamber. We need to get out of here.

If we can get out.

'Ferdy?' I look up at the other door. 'Where does that lead?'

Ferdy is still holding Anna's hand. 'Rigor mortis sets in approximately three hours after death and—'

'Ferdy? Listen to me!'

'—lasts approximately twelve hours.' He looks at the door. 'Ferdy doesn't know.'

I press my face against the metal bars. I can feel cold air, but I don't feel a breeze. Glancing back to the other door, all I can see is fallen rock and debris. That way is completely impassable. I focus on the door and push it out of its hinges. It falls to the floor beyond with a crash.

A sea of darkness lies beyond the chamber. Ferdy is suddenly by my side. He presses his head against my shoulder.

'Do you know where this leads?' I ask.

'We are only a hundred feet from the ocean,' he says. 'Jellyfish have no heart or brain.'

'Okay. That's handy to know.'

A light suddenly flicks on, illuminating the inky blackness. Ferdy has a torch. Thank God for small miracles. I take it from him and shine it around the interior. At first it looks like things have gone from bad to worse. We're standing in some sort of naturally occurring cave. The ceiling at the back seems to gradually slope down to the floor.

There is a pile of rocks and debris to our left. I hold onto Ferdy's arm while we examine the debris. If I was expecting a secret tunnel or an elevator leading upwards, I'm very sadly mistaken. There's nothing back here.

A tiny ping interrupts the silence.

I look back towards the rear of the cave where the ceiling meets the floor. It is as smooth as glass.

Water.

'Ferdy. Is that a pool?' I ask.

'The speed of light is two hundred and ninety-nine—'

'Yeah, that's great, but is—Oh, never mind.'

I kneel down and touch my hand to the liquid. It is dead cold to the touch. Tasting it, my hopes rise.

'Salt,' I say. 'Ferdy, this is salt water.'

'We are only one hundred feet from the ocean,' Ferdy says.

Holy hell.

This is what Ferdy has been trying to tell me.

'Is this an underground river? Does it lead to the ocean?'

'David Blane broke the world record when he held his breath for seventeen minutes and four seconds—'

'Hopefully we won't have to break his record.'

I turn off the torch. At first all I can see is dark, but after several seconds I'm aware of a faint glow coming from the back of the still lake. I turn the torch back on.

'Ferdy?' I get down on my knees and look into his face. 'You understand what we have to do? We have to swim through the water to the other side. Can you swim?'

'The world record for backstroke is—'

'Can you swim?'

'The deepest part of the earth's oceans is the Marianas Trench—'

'That's great.' I let out a deep sigh. 'Ferdy.

We have to get out of here. I'm going to swim through under the water till I reach the ocean. You have to hold onto my belt. With your other hand I need you to light the way. Hopefully the torch will hold out. Do you understand?'

'The deepest part of the trench—' He stops. 'Ferdy understands.'

I stare into his eyes. I hope he does. I think he's autistic, but it's a special type of autism where he has unlimited amounts of knowledge. He needs to understand that he cannot let go of me in the water. If he does, I'll probably never find him again. For that matter, if the torch should fail we'll drown in the dark or if I can't hold my breath long enough—

I latch his hand onto the back of my belt and explain to him again what I'm going to do. He still seems to look straight through me, but he nods occasionally as I speak. Finally I step into the water and he obediently follows me into the cold, clear fluid. We walk until it rises to my waist.

'We need to take deep breaths, Ferdy. Do you understand?'

He nods.

'We're going to take three deep breaths and then we'll dive in. We're going to swim until we reach the ocean on the other side. Okay?'

'Okay,' he says. '*Pictichromis diadema* are a type of fish.'

'I'll keep that in mind.' We take another step into the water. 'Take a deep breath. That's it. And number two. Yes. And now…three!'

The black water closes in around us.

Chapter Thirty-Seven

We are lost in an endless void of black. It's impossible to tell up from down. It's only the trail of bubbles trickling from my mouth that show the difference. The water is freezing. And motionless. A cold deep well into which we have fallen and from which there is no reprieve.

The roof of the cave angles deeper and deeper into the water and we follow it all the way down into the icy depths. Certainly the water flows from the ocean into this small cave, but by what circuitous path? How many twists and turns before we reach the end? How deep must we dive before we can rise again?

The rock face aims ever downwards.

It occurs to me that I should have used our powers to aid us, but my training with Mr Brown did not include underwater activities. There's only one direction to go. And that's down.

Ferdy hangs onto my belt ever more tightly as my eyes begin to bulge from the pressure. The rock face angles away from me.

It continues downwards. My chest is beginning to feel the crush of the pressure. My brain and millions of years of evolution tell me I should breathe. Yet I have to hold my breath. My body is being denied of oxygen, the one element it should be able to master. I swim harder downwards.

Abruptly, like the edge of a knife, the rock comes to a halt. I pull us around and we start to ascend. We head up ten feet. Twenty feet. Thirty feet.

Something is wrong. My arms and legs are in such a flurry of activity to project me forward that it has taken me several seconds to realize I am missing something vitally important.

Light.

Why can't I see any light?

If I have come up on the other side of an enormous boulder, why am I not seeing a cave beyond and the glow of the outside world? I am seriously running out of air. My lungs are pounding. My heart is racketing along like a steam train. Why can't I see any light?

Because I'm in a cave.

And now there is only one way to find light. That is to extinguish it so I reach down and grip the torch in Ferdy's hand and shut my eyes tightly. When I open them I see a translucent column of light growing out of the darkness.

I snap the torch back on. Ferdy must be feeling the need for air as keenly as me. Possibly it is only his autism—or whatever his ailment is—that has stopped him from panicking. I swim as hard as I can towards the spot where I spotted the faint flow. A bubble of air involuntarily escapes from my mouth and I snort in a nose full of salty brine.

I swim even harder and the water seems to press against my brain. If I don't make it in the next few seconds *we are both going to drown.*

The column of light arcs down towards us from above.

Yes!

I can see a gap in the rock.

We are going to make it!

The column of light cuts through the water

like sunlight carving a path through storm clouds to illuminate the landscape below. It draws me to the gap between the rocks. From here, I can see the surface of the water. It lies between two parallel boulders wedged about five inches apart from each other. My arm shoots up and the rest of me follows. I bang my head against one of the rocks and with that final stab of pain I realize I can't fit through the gap.

It is even too narrow for Ferdy.

Oh God, what have I done?

I need to focus on using the air above to push the rocks aside, but the lack of air is turning the world black around me. We are drowning and there is nothing I can do. I need to create a wedge between the rocks, but black spots are drowning my vision.

Ferdy releases my belt and pushes past my body. He feels the gap between the two rocks. Everything is turning inky black. I have failed him and failed myself. I need to concentrate. Somehow bring air down from above into my mouth and lungs.

But I can't!

The water *rumbles* around me. As the liquid

pushes into my nose I see Ferdy shoving the two boulders aside. I raise my arm. Ferdy grabs it and hauls me up from the water. I lie like a beached fish, coughing and spluttering and choking and spitting out salt water.

Air. Glorious air.

My face presses hard against the gritty rock face. We are at the entrance to a cave pointing onto the ocean. I can see briny seaweed. Tiny mollusks dot the slimy rock face. A crab sidles out of sight. The cave opens out onto a rock platform that follows the coast away into the distance.

I roll over to see Ferdy standing over me with a curious expression.

'Ferdy.' My first attempt at communication is unsuccessful; I spend the next minute vomiting up more seawater. 'Ferdy. Did you move the rock?'

'Rock?'

He picks up a boulder as large as a small cow and throws it fifty feet into the waters beyond. It skips across the ocean a few times before it sinks from sight forever. I stagger to my feet.

'An octopus has three hearts,' Ferdy tells me.

'Really? How interesting.'

Obviously, Ferdy not only has a super brain, but he also has super strength.

I spend the next few minutes telling him I have to leave for a while, but I'll be back later. Trying to go into more detail would be a waste of time. I consider urging him to be careful and don't talk to strangers, but somehow I think Ferdy can look after himself.

Chapter Thirty-Eight

I fly low over the landscape back towards The Agency complex. I do it just as Mr Brown trained me. I stay low to keep off the radar. I come in to land near one of the bunkers, angle one of the cameras away from me and use a hard clot of air to unlock the door.

The stairwell embraces me. A few minutes later I'm making my way through the corridors of the main complex. Soon I'm crossing The Cavern. Administrative personnel and scientists are everywhere, but I'm looking for one man.

There's no doubt in my mind most of the staff here don't know what's been going on. How could they? The Agency works like most secret organizations. Everything is on a need to know basis only. There are a hundred projects taking place at any one time. But there are some people who know. They've always known what was intended for us; the experiments, the abuse, the deaths.

And one man has certainly known right from the start.

I make my way to our dorm rooms first. I hope to get the others behind me before I go on the attack, but they're nowhere to be found. A sense of disquiet seizes me. Maybe they're out partying. Or maybe on some impromptu training exercise.

Or maybe they've been ambushed like me.

When I return to The Cavern I spot Mr Jones stepping out of an elevator. His eyes widen slightly when he sees me. It's his only giveaway, but it's all I need. I grab him and push him back through the elevator doors. They slide shut behind us.

'You've known all along?' I ask him. 'Haven't you?'

'I don't know what you're—'

His reply is suddenly choked off.

I tell him. 'It's hard to speak without air. The vocal chords don't work. The lungs refuse to function.'

He tries to grab me, but I use my powers to force his arms down by his side. Then I hit the emergency stop button for the elevator.

'How long can the average person survive

without air?' I ask. 'Someone told me the world record is seventeen minutes. How long do you think you'll last?'

Jones looks at me in horror as he starts to suffocate. Finally he shakes his head from side to side. His eyes fill with terror.

'You want to speak?'

He nods energetically.

'Really? And you're going to tell me the truth?'

A kind of pathetic horror comes into his eyes.

I release him and he falls gasping to the floor. His hand makes for his jacket.

'Don't even think about it,' I warn him. 'I can crush you like an ant.'

I don't actually know if I can crush him like an ant, but it's a good line.

He gasps. 'What do you want?'

'Where is Twelve?' I ask. 'Where are my friends?'

'They're in the main lab on Level Fourteen.'

'Why?'

'I don't know.'

I force his arms back to his sides. 'Please,' he begs. 'I really don't know. I think he's lost it. He said he needs to carry out more experiments, but—'

'But what?'

'He's not a scientist,' Jones says desperately. 'What could he possibly be doing?'

What could he be doing?

That's the sixty-four million dollar question. I don't know what you get when you combine an alien without ethics, a lab full of potent mixtures and a collection of human guinea pigs. It's a terrifying thought. I hit the elevator button and it sinks down into the earth.

The elevator draws to a halt and the doors open. I grip Mr Jones by the arm and draw him close.

'We're going for a little walk down the corridor,' I tell him. 'If you make so much of a squeak, I'm going to tear your head off. Do you understand?'

'Yes.'

'You're going to lead me to this lab,' I say.

'Let's move.'

We make our way down the corridor. Two scientists pass by and give us a long glance, but say nothing. It's Mr Jones who gets us through; he must have the clearance to get into just about every part of The Agency.

'I want you to know I was against these experiments,' he pleads. 'I've got kids of my own. Why would I want to harm—'

'Shut up.'

He shuts up. We reach the door of a lab and Jones takes out a swipe card. The door clicks open. We shuttle inside.

Brodie, Chad, Dan and Ebony are lying unconscious on lab tables. I release Jones and grip Chad's wrist. Thank God. A faint pulse. He's still alive. My eyes scan the lab. There is equipment all around. Pieces of machinery fill every corner. Dark shadows hide benches of test tubes, beakers and gadgetry I don't understand.

This is where we were born.

Correction.

This is where we were *reborn*.

The alien known as Twelve steps from the shadows.

He's laughing. Actually laughing.

'What's all this about?' I ask.

'Do you know how long I've been watching your race?' he asks. 'I've been stuck on this insignificant little world at the back end of the galaxy for over two thousand years. I've watched, steered you away from your animalistic natures, and you know what I've realized?

'I don't want to. There's something…alluring about humans. The way you happily kill and mutilate and torture each other. It's strangely intoxicating.' He shakes his head. 'Oh, the other Bakari don't share my beliefs. In fact, they're in the process of having me replaced. Can you imagine? I'm returning home after two thousand years.

'Guess what? I don't want to go.' Twelve laughs. 'I'm more human than Bakari now! I wanted Doctor Richards to turn me into the ultimate human! Can you imagine? A human who can kill and destroy with ease, tearing apart anything in his way?'

'But when I told Doctor Richards my intentions he thought me mad! He and the other scientists stole you away from here so that you would be safe! We only caught up with them again when we realized they were using Cygnus Industries—one of our safe houses—as a meeting point.

'But Typhoid was ahead of us. They wanted the secrets of The Alpha Project too.'

'You have your formula,' I tell him. 'Just let me and my friends go!'

'Don't you understand?' Twelve screams. 'We no longer have the formula. Richards destroyed it before leaving the base. The remaining batches he mixed together so that we could never replicate it again.'

His face cracks into a leer. 'All the formulas. Mixed together. Do you know what that means?'

Actually, I don't. I glance over at Jones and even he looks terrified. I'm beginning to realize that Twelve has not just exceeded his authority, but also his reason. Somewhere along the line he has crossed the fine boundary between sanity and madness.

'Did you really think we would leave such power in the hands of children?' he asks.

Twelve curls his hand into a fist and holds it out in front of him. He unravels it and stares at his palm.

He's lost it completely, I think.

But then a tiny flame appears in the palm of his hand. It grows into a white ball of fire, hot and bright in the dimly lit laboratory. With sudden horror I begin to understand what he has done.

'You've drunk some of the remaining formula,' I say.

'No.' The alien begins to laugh. 'I've drunk *all* of it.'

Chapter Thirty-Nine

He flings the flame at me and I leap to one side. The ball of fire strikes the wall behind me. I hear Jones scream and see him race to the open door.

'Run!' Twelve thunders at him as he disappears through the doorway. 'Run and tell them a God has come to earth!'

Oh dear.

Twelve has been reading too many comic books.

He leaps over a table and cartwheels over a bench. I can't let him touch me. If he has everyone's combined powers then he has Ebony's transmutation ability. He could turn me to dust in seconds.

I create a force shield between us and he collides with it. He points at me and a jagged band of ice tries to reach through the shield.

Damn, he's strong.

'They will build a statue to me!' he snarls.

I don't care about statues. Instead, I focus on removing his air supply. Suddenly he finds out what life without oxygen is like. At the same time I leap over a table and through the exit door. While we're fighting in the lab the others are in danger. I need to get him away from them and out into the open.

Racing down the corridor I keep a shield up behind me, but Twelve doesn't follow. Mr Jones is already gone. I jump into an elevator and hit the button for The Cavern. There's plenty of room up there.

The elevator shudders violently. I look down at my feet. It took me some time to get used to flying. Is it possible that—

A fist slams through the floor.

Damn!

Twelve's enraged face appears through the jagged tear in the floor.

'You will obey me, child!'

I send a wall of wind at him that takes out the entire floor. The elevator—or what remains of it—continues to rise. I destroy its ceiling and fly past the useless cable. Down below Twelve has fallen several floors and punched a hole in one of the walls to stop his descent.

Zooming past several floors I reach ground level and force air molecules between the doors. A sound comes rushing towards me as I throw myself through the gap.

A ball of white hot fire screams up the elevator shaft and out of sight. I hear an explosion and screaming. The ground shudders. Sirens start sounding throughout the complex. Fire alarms come to life. I fly across a sea of machinery.

Another explosion sounds from the direction of the shaft. Landing, I look back and see an enormous piece of machinery flying through the air. It slams into a number of scientists scattering for cover.

No!

I take to the air again. I've got to take Twelve out as quickly as possible. He is completely out of control. Whereas I have compunctions about taking a human life, he is clearly beyond caring about such trivialities. I build up a blast force of air, but before I can hurl it at him he fires a column of ice at me and I am instantly encased within a block of ice.

Cold.

It's so damn cold.

I am completely enclosed within a frozen coffin. Even before I hit the floor the block of ice has expanded so rapidly it has become several feet thick. It is almost worse than drowning; I am unable to move at all.

Yet, that's not completely true. There is the tiniest space between my body and the ice. It's not even a sixteenth of an inch, but I think it might be enough. I focus on that tiny pocket of air. I make it search out for a weakness in the ice. It finds a tiny crack near my pelvis. It breaks into that crack and expands it like a stone cutter smashing open a rock with a single blow.

Cracckkk!

The ice explodes into a thousand pieces. I'm just in time to see a look of astonishment on the alien's face before I wipe away the expression with a blast of hurricane wind that knocks him flying.

A hail of bullets ring out just as Twelve

regains his feet.

Damn.

Fortunately they're aimed at Twelve. Unfortunately, they don't make a mark. Obviously his alien makeup also gives him some sort of super tough skin. How quickly we become obsolete. While Twelve is distracted I pick up a bench and decide to use it as a club. As I bring it around to take off the alien's head, he swings about and grabs it in mid air.

He turns it to white powder.

That's a problem. Anything I hit him with is just going to dissolve into some chemical compound. Unless I throw so many things at him at once that he can't focus on them all simultaneously.

Within seconds I've got dozens of items flying through the air at him. I see a cut open up over his left eye. Okay. I'm getting somewhere now. His invulnerability is dependent on his focus. If he is kept busy, he can't focus on protecting himself.

A person races across the concourse towards Twelve. At first I think it's a guard trying to attack him. Then I realize it's Mr Evans, Twelve's receptionist.

'No!' I yell. 'Keep back from him!'

Through some misguided loyalty, Evans has decided to try to make Twelve see reason.

There's nothing I can do. The aide has already reached the alien. Twelve looks up to see the man and laughs. It is the delusional cackle of a madman. The expression on Evans' face falters.

'Get back!' I scream.

Twelve steps forward. 'I want to thank you for all your years of service, Mr Evans.'

He grabs the aide and turns him to a yellow powder. Sulphur. The person that was Mr Evans *splats* to the floor. Now Twelve returns his attention to me.

He blasts me with another beam of fire. I only just get my shield up in time. This time the heat is so intense I can't concentrate on staying in the air. I hit the floor and curl up into a ball as I struggle to keep my barrier in place. Twelve is directing some sort of nova blast at me, a heat so intense it's seeping through the barrier.

I should have flown away, I think. *Now it's too late.*

At that instant the blast ends. The floor all around me is scorched and burning. I expect to see Twelve advancing on me, but instead he is lying on the floor about ten feet away. He is badly burnt.

What has happened?

A voice rings out from my right.

'You take on one of us,' Chad yells. 'You take on all of us!'

Chapter Forty

Chad!

I never thought I would actually be pleased to see him. The others suddenly appear from behind a pile of smoldering equipment.

'We leave you alone for five minutes…' Brodie starts.

'We need to move this fight out of here,' I interrupt.

I look past them and spy the break in the roof for the aircraft to depart. Dan is one step ahead of me. Within seconds he has torn it apart and light is steaming into The Cavern. I build a flying ramp to take us through the gap. No sooner are we through than a bolt of ice flies past.

'He's been doing that all day,' I tell them.

'What the hell's going on?' Chad asks.

I give them the abridged version. 'So he's got all our powers. And then some. I'm not sure how we can put him out of commission.'

'Don't forget we have something he doesn't

have,' Brodie points out.

'What's that?'

'Experience,' she says. 'Thanks to the last few weeks we know how to control our powers. He doesn't. He almost blew himself up with that last blast of fire.'

Something comes flying out through the gap in the ground. We watch it soar over our heads and hit the earth about twenty feet behind us.

It's some sort of tank.

'How much of that juice did he drink?' Dan asks.

Twelve flies through the opening and lands awkwardly on the grass before us.

'You children are finished!' he snarls.

'Hey Twelve!' Ebony calls out. 'Get some new lines. You sound like you're out of some bad comic book.'

We look at Ebony with new respect. I'm just about to make a really snappy follow up when Twelve levitates a metal bench from the cavern. He swings it around like a child swinging a toy. Just as it's about to collide with Brodie, she leaps out of the way. Dan is not so lucky. It catches him a glancing blow and knocks him flying.

Chad drags him out of the way.

'I think my foot is broken,' he groans.

We need to co-ordinate our efforts. It's too late to have a meeting to formulate a plan, so we need something simple. Something with which we're already familiar. An idea comes to me in a flash.

'The island!' I yell. 'The same as the island.'

Chad and Dan move away from us. Dan raises a piece of metallic debris and uses it as a shield while Chad fires alternating bursts of fire and ice at Twelve. I gather up Brodie and Ebony and we take up position behind the alien. So far the plan's working. The boys have created a diversion. Now we just need to trap Twelve. Permanently.

'I can get his attention,' Brodie says.

'Will I make a hole?' Ebony asks.

'Yes,' I tell her. 'We just need to make him lie in it.'

Brodie grabs up a piece of debris, a thin shaft

of metal that has flown off one of the pieces of equipment. She hefts it experimentally in her right arm.

'I'm ready when you are,' she says.

'Hey Twelve!' I yell.

The boys momentarily stop their bombardment. Twelve swings around as Brodie flings the makeshift javelin with all her might. It strikes the alien across the eyes. He flinches. At the same moment Ebony drops to her knees.

A hole, thirty feet across and twenty feet deep, forms under the alien. He falls into the pit. Using all my power, I somehow drag the tank—or whatever it is—into the air. It hovers over the hole.

'Chad!' I scream.

He understands instantly.

As I drop the device, Chad directs a molten blast at the metal. Whatever it is turns to molten liquid and slaps into the base of the pit. There is a single, brief scream from below us that dies into a horrible silence. We hesitantly make our way to the edge and look in.

The metal is still cooling, but at the center of the molten liquid there is the figure of a man. He looks like some sort of heroic figure. Almost like something out of Greek mythology.

'He said there would be a statue,' I muse. 'I don't think that's what he meant.'

Chapter Forty-One

'But you can't just leave,' Mr Jones tries to tell us.

We have found a campervan parked in one of the underground car parks. It's quite modern. Must be worth a fortune. Unlike the one we arrived in, this one has windows and bedding for everyone. This will be our home.

For now, anyway.

'Try and stop us,' Chad suggests.

After seeing us fight Twelve to a standstill, the idea obviously does not appeal to Mr Jones.

While we're talking, we're packing our few belongings into the van. There's precious little. The Agency took away our names, our homes, our families. Everything that identified us as who we were. The Agency took almost everything away from us.

All we have left now is each other.

'I'm not sanctioning what Twelve did,' Mr Jones says. 'I *can't* sanction what he did. The other branches of The Agency are up in arms over it. They're completely disavowing Twelve's actions. It's a complete betrayal of everything for which The Agency stands.'

'I'm glad to hear you say that,' I replied.

It's hard to know what's true and what's a lie. Mr Jones and some of the others at The Agency knew about The Alpha Project. Trying to prove it or track down all those in charge would be a pointless exercise. Doctor Richards destroyed all the records and the death of Twelve signaled the final end to the whole experiment.

Mr Jones has already told us that a replacement is being brought in for Twelve. He has said there will be more accountability for projects within The Agency. Personally, I don't care. I'm just glad we're getting out of here.

We're taking the campervan. Now we just want to be left alone to make our own place in the world. If we can.

Just before we start our journey, Mr Jones makes one last attempt to stop us.

'I understand why you're upset.' He tries to be conciliatory. 'And the last thing I would ever want to do is threaten you.'

'Yes?'

'You may have forgotten those poisonous capsules we implanted in your bodies?'

I reach into my pocket. 'Oh? You mean these?'

His jaw drops as I hand them to him.

'They were difficult to find,' I tell him. 'But fortunately they're made from metal and Dan has a special affinity for metallic substances.'

'You mean—'

'It was painful,' I tell Jones. 'But he got them out.'

Mr Jones makes one final attempt. 'But we've invested an enormous amount in you!'

I climb into the driver's seat and wind the window down. 'And we're going to pay you back. By not exposing you to the world and by not suing your organization through the International Court of Justice.'

'You can't threaten us!'

'Let's see,' I begin. 'Kidnapping, child endangerment, abuse, deprivation of liberty…'

'And that's just for starters,' Chad climbs into the seat next to me. 'I've got all these injuries that need fixing. I need compensation for my sore knee. My elbow…'

'I'm not saying you'll never see us again,' I tell Mr Jones. I'm thinking of Pegasus and what would have happened if we had not stopped Typhoid. The world needs super heroes. Even teenage superheroes like us. 'If you ever need us, really need us, we're prepared to help.'

Chad vigorously shakes his head. 'Speak for yourself. I'm never coming back.'

I raise an eyebrow at Mr Jones and shrug.

'Where will I find you?' he asks.

I look up the road. 'Where does this lead?'

His eyes follow the road into the distance.

I nod. 'That's where you'll find us.'

Epilog

We have driven all through the day and all through the night. Putting as much distance between us and The Agency seems to be the only thing that makes sense. The others are asleep. Only I am awake as I maneuver the motor home across the desert. We're passing through Monument Valley, one of the beautiful parts of the United States. We're on our way to the Grand Canyon. I've never been there.

Or if I have, I don't remember it.

Last night I had that dream again. It's the one where I'm in a field of wheat. I'm running my hands through the tall grass and walking towards a farmhouse. There's someone sitting on the step. It's a boy.

I think it's my brother.

Maybe he's still alive. Maybe he's waiting for me. Maybe my parents are still alive too. For all I know, there's a family sitting around a dinner table awaiting my return.

I don't believe anything Mr Jones said. How

can I? Solomon Wolff told us the Bakari are not the only aliens on Earth. There are others. Who knows what their agenda is?

My eyes scan past the ageless rock formations and I see the last stars are fading from the night sky. The horizon is growing lighter by the moment. Now the sun is about to crest the sky. Dawn is only a few minutes away. Soon it will be another day.

There is movement at my side and someone climbs into the seat next to me.

Brodie.

'Pull over for a moment,' she says. 'It's important.'

Who am I to deny a beautiful girl?

Bringing the vehicle over to the edge, we both climb out and look across the desert. It will be hot later and the air will swim with moisture, but for now it is cool and motionless. A quiet, peaceful place. Peaceful is good.

She pulls out a book. It's the one Doctor Richards handed to me back in the hotel room. The book with all the blank pages. It seems like a million years since I last looked at it. I stare at it stupidly as she hands it to me.

'Open it,' she instructs.

I flip open to a page in the middle. It is as blank as any other. Now Brodie produces the strange device we found buried in the spine of the book.

'That Ferdy's amazing,' she says. 'He spent five minutes playing with this thing and had it all worked out.'

She grips the glass tightly, then suddenly seems to twist it in both directions at once. It clicks and a pale beam of light shines from it.

'How did you do that?'

'Don't worry about how,' she advises. 'Just look.'

I hold the glass over the page. Where I look through I can see words written on the paper. It's like some sort of infrared light that makes the writing visible. I can see formula written on the pages. And addresses.

Addresses.

Our homes?

The homes of our families?

'What...how—'

I can't speak and that becomes even more difficult as Brodie grabs the book from me and presses her lips against mine.

'Like I said,' Brodie draws back. 'That Ferdy's a bright kid.'

We kiss again as a gentle breeze tilts at the air. After a while, we return to the van and I start the engine. We've all been through so much. We've all come such a long way. I need to write all this down. I need to keep a diary. It's not every teenager that becomes a super hero.

But first things first. My stomach rumbles. We'll need to eat soon. That's another crisis we need to sort out. I was able to convince Mr Jones to supply us with some funds, but all that is now gone.

'We need money,' I tell Brodie as we drive through the desert. 'We need to get some food.'

'Oh, we'll be fine.'

'Yeah?'

She holds up a rose. A perfect rose in every

way. I remember seeing Ebony with it the previous day at one of the rest stops. She was saying how lovely it would be to preserve it forever.

Now it is made from gold.

Solid gold.

'Money won't be a problem,' Brodie says.

Laughing, we drive into the dawn.

A Few Final Words

I hope you enjoyed reading Diary of a Teenage Superhero. It is the first book in the Teen Superheroes series. There are many more to enjoy! The other books are:

The Doomsday Device (Book 2)

The Battle for Earth (Book 3)

The Twisted Future (Book 4)

Terminal Fear (Book 5)

I love hearing from my readers. You can contact me at darrellpitt@gmail.com

Thanks again and happy reading!

Darrell

CPSIA information can be obtained
at www.ICGtesting.com
Printed in the USA
BVOW06s1722050317
477803BV00011B/276/P